## Praise for *Ayiti*

"[Haiti's] better scribes, among them Edwidge Danticat, Frankétienne, Madison Smartt Bell, Lyonel Trouillot, and Marie Vieux Chauvet, have produced some of the best literature in the world. Add to their ranks Roxane Gay, a bright and shining star. *Ayiti* is an exciting new chapter in an old and beautiful story."

—Kyle Minor, author of *In the Devil's Territory*

"These are powerful stories written with verve and there's this great sense at the collection's close that nothing will stop the Haitian people, the human spirit, or Roxane Gay."

—Ethel Rohan, author of *The Weight of Him*

"A set of brief, tart stories mostly set amid the Haitian-American community and circling around themes of violation, abuse, and heartbreak . . . This book set the tone that still characterizes much of Gay's writing: clean, unaffected, allowing the (often furious) emotions to rise naturally out of calm, declarative sentences. That gives her briefest stories a punch even when they come in at two pages or fewer, sketching out the challenges of assimilation in terms of accents, meals, or 'What You Need to Know About a Haitian Woman.' . . . This debut amply contains the righteous energy that drives all her work."

—*Kirkus Reviews*

## Praise for *Difficult Women* and Roxane Gay

"There's a distinct echo of Angela Carter or Helen Oyeyemi at play; dark fables and twisted morality tales sit alongside the contemporary and the realistic."

*—Los Angeles Times*

"Gay's signature dry wit and piercing psychological depth make every story mesmerizingly unusual and simply unforgettable." *—Harper's Bazaar*

"Writing that seems to cut to the bone."

*—Seattle Times*

"Like Joyce Carol Oates' *Where Are You Going, Where Have You Been?* or Shirley Jackson's *We Have Always Lived in the Castle*, this is fiction pressed through a sieve, leaving only the canniest truths behind . . . Addictive, moving and risk-taking."

*—San Francisco Chronicle*

"Roxane Gay . . . charges from the gate . . . These are the places I'm going to take you, Gay seems to be saying. Are you prepared?" *—Globe and Mail* (Canada)

"Roxane Gay is a force." *—Rumpus*

"[Gay's] goodness cuts to the quick of human experience. Her work returns again and again to issues of power, the body, desire, trauma, survival, truth."

*—Brooklyn Magazine*

# ayiti

Also by Roxane Gay

FICTION
*An Untamed State*
*Difficult Women*

NONFICTION
*Bad Feminist: Essays*
*Hunger: A Memoir of (My) Body*

# ayiti

## ROXANE GAY

**Grove Press**
*New York*

*Published simultaneously in Canada*
*Printed in the United States of America*

This book set in 12 pt. Warnock Pro
by Alpha Design & Composition of Pittsfield, NH

First published by Artistically Declined Press: October 2011
First Grove Atlantic edition: June 2018

ISBN 978-0-8021-2826-3
eISBN 978-0-8021-6573-2

Library of Congress Cataloging-in-Publication data
is available for this title.

Grove Press
an imprint of Grove Atlantic
154 West 14th Street
New York, NY 10011

Distributed by Publishers Group West

groveatlantic.com

18 19 20 21    10 9 8 7 6 5 4 3 2 1

*For my mother and father*

# Contents

# CONTENTS

# Motherfuckers

Gérard spends his days thinking about the many reasons he hates America that include but are not limited to the people, the weather, especially the cold, and having to drive everywhere and having to go to school every day. He is fourteen. He hates lots of things.

On the first day of school, as he and his classmates introduce themselves, Gérard stands, says his name, quickly sits back down, and stares at his desk, which he hates. "You have such an interesting accent," the teacher coos. "Where are you from?" He looks up. He is irritated. "Haiti," he says. The teacher smiles widely. "Say something in French." Gérard complies. "Je te déteste," he says. The teacher claps excitedly. She doesn't speak French.

Word spreads through school quickly and soon, Gérard has a nickname. His classmates call him HBO.

It is several weeks until he understands what that means.

Gérard lives with his parents in a two-bedroom apartment. He shares his room with his sister and their cousin Edy. They do not have cable television, but Edy, who has been in the States for several months longer than Gérard, lies and tells him that HBO is Home Box Office, a TV channel that shows Bruce Willis movies. Gérard hates that they don't have cable but loves Bruce Willis. He is proud of his nickname. When the kids at school call him HBO, he replies, "Yippee-ki-yay."

Gérard's father does not shower every day because he has yet to become accustomed to indoor plumbing. Instead, he performs his ablutions each morning at the bathroom sink and reserves the luxury of a shower for weekends. Sometimes, Gérard sits on the edge of the bathtub and watches his father because it reminds him of home. He has the routine memorized—his father splashes his armpits with water, then lathers with soap, then rinses, then draws a damp washcloth across his chest, the back of his neck, behind his ears. His father excuses Gérard, then washes between his thighs. He finishes his routine by washing his face and brushing his teeth. Then he goes to work. Back home, he was a journalist. In the States, he slices meat at a deli counter for eight hours a day and pretends not to speak English fluently.

In the second month of school, Gérard finds a bag of cheap colognes in his locker. "For HBO" is written on the front of the bag in large block letters. It is a strange gift, he thinks, and he hates the way the bag smells but he takes it home. Edy rolls his eyes when Gérard shows his cousin his gift, but takes one of the bottles of cologne. His girlfriend will enjoy it. "Those motherfuckers," Edy says. He is far more skilled at cursing in English. Then Edy explains what HBO means. Gérard clenches his fists. He decides that he hates each and every motherfucker he goes to school with. The next morning, he applies cologne so liberally that it makes his classmates' eyes water.

When they call him HBO, he adds a little something extra to his yippee-ki-yay.

# About My
# Father's Accent

He knows it's there. He knows it's thick, thicker even than my mother's. He's been on American soil for nearly thirty years, but his voice sounds like Port-au-Prince, the crowded streets, the blaring horns, the smell of grilled meat and roasting corn, the heat, thick and still.

In his voice, we hear him climbing coconut trees, gripping the trunk with his bare feet and sandy legs, cutting coconuts down with a dull machete. We hear him dancing to konpa, the palm of one hand resting against his belly, his other hand raised high in the air as he rocks his hips from side to side. We hear him telling us about Toussaint L'Ouverture and Henri Christophe and the pride of being first free black. We hear the taste of bitterness when he watches the news from home or calls those left behind.

When we, my brothers and I, mimic him, he smiles indulgently. Before every vowel an "h," at the end of every plural, no "s."

"You make fun, but you understand me perfectly, don't you?" he says. We nod. We ask him to say American Airlines. We gasp for air when he gives in.

For many years, we didn't realize our parents had accents, that their voices sounded different to unkind American ears. All we heard was home.

Then the world intruded. It always does.

# Voodoo Child

When my college roommate learns I am Haitian, she is convinced I practice voodoo, thanks to the Internet in the hands of the feeble-minded. I do nothing to dissuade her fears even though I was raised Catholic and have gained my inadequate understanding of voodoo from the Lisa Bonet movie that made Bill Cosby mad at her as if he had the nerve to be mad at anyone about anything.

In the middle of the night, I chant mysteriously, light candles. By day, I wear red and white, paint my face, dance possessed. I leave a doll on my desk. It looks just like my roommate. The doll is covered with strategically placed pins. I like fucking with her. She gives me the bigger room with the better dresser. She offers to take my tray to the dish room in the dining hall.

We take the bus to Manhattan to shop and dance and drink and hook up with dirty New York boys. I am the devil she knows.

As we emerge from Grand Central, a large, older woman runs up to me, grabs my arm, starts bowing furiously.

My mother always told me: back away slowly from crazy people; they are everywhere. When she first came to the States, she had to live in the worst part of the Bronx, the part of that borough burned beyond recognition. She hasn't yet recovered.

There, in front of Grand Central, my roommate clung to my arm, her fingers digging deep, drawing blood, as if I were better equipped to handle the situation.

As we backed away, I realized the woman was speaking in Creole. I didn't know her but I knew her. "Ki sa ou vle?" I asked her. She told me I was a famous mambo. She said it was such a pleasure to see me in America. She grabbed my wrists. She kissed my palms, held them to her cheeks. She wanted, I think, to be blessed. I was still imagining all the dirty New York boys my roommate and I would later find.

# There Is No "E" in Zombi, Which Means There Can Be No You or We

[A Primer]


[Things Americans do not know about zombis:]
    They are not dead. They are near death.
        There's a difference.
    They are not imaginary.
    They do not eat human flesh.
    They cannot eat salt.
    They do not walk around with their arms
        and legs locked stiffly.
    They can be saved.


[How you pronounce zombi:]
    Zaahhhhnnnnnn-bee. You have to feel it in
        the roof your mouth, let it vibrate.
        Say it fast.
    The "m" is silent. Sort of.

[How to make a zombi:]
    You need a good reason, a very good reason.
    You need a puffer fish, and a small sample of blood
        and hair from your chosen candidate.
    Instructions: Kill the puffer fish. Don't be squea-
        mish. Extract the poison. Just find a way. Allow
        it to dry. Grind it with the blood and hair to
        create your coup de poudre. A good chemist
        can help. Blow the powder into the candidate's
        face. Wait.


[A love story]


Micheline Bérnard always loved Lionel Desormeaux. Their parents were friends though that bonhomie had not quite carried on to the children. Micheline and Lionel went to primary and secondary school together, had known each other all their lives— when Lionel looked upon Micheline he was always overcome with the vague feeling he had seen her somewhere before while she was overcome with the precise knowledge that he was the man of her dreams. In truth, everyone loved Lionel Desormeaux. He was tall and brown with high cheekbones and full lips. His body was perfectly muscled and after a long day of swimming in the ocean, he would emerge from the salty water, glistening. Micheline would sit in a cabana, invisible. She would lick her lips and she would stare. She would think, "Look at me, Lionel," but he never did.

When Lionel walked, there was an air about him. He moved slowly but with deliberate steps and sometimes, as he walked, people swore they could hear the bass of a deep drum. His mother, who loved her only boy more than any other, always told him, "Lionel, you are the son of L'Ouverture." He believed her. He believed everything his mother ever told him. Lionel always told his friends, "My father freed our people. I am his greatest son."

In Port-au-Prince, there were too many women. Micheline knew competition for Lionel's attention was fierce. She was attractive, petite. She wore her thick hair in a sensible bun. On weekends, she would let that hair down and when she walked by, men would shout, "Quelle belle paire de jambes," what beautiful legs, and Micheline would savor the thrilling taste of their attention. Most Friday nights, Micheline and her friends gathered at Oasis, a popular nightclub on the edge of the Bel Air slum. She drank fruity drinks and smoked French cigarettes and wore skirts revealing just the right amount of leg. Lionel was always surrounded by a mob of adoring women. He let them buy him rum and Cokes and always sat at the center of the room wearing his pressed linen slacks and dark T-shirts that showed off his perfect, chiseled arms. At the end of the night, he would select one woman to take home, bed her thoroughly, and wish her well the following morning. The stone path to his front door was lined with the salted tears and soiled panties of the women Lionel had sexed then scorned.

On her birthday, Micheline decided she would be the woman Lionel took home that night. She wore a bright sundress, strapless. She dabbed perfume everywhere she wanted to feel Lionel's lips. She wore heels so high her brother had to help her into the nightclub. When Lionel arrived to hold court, Micheline made sure she was closest. She smiled widely and angled her shoulders just so and leaned in so he could see everything he wanted to see of her ample cleavage. At the end of the night, Lionel nodded in her direction. He said, "Tonight, my dear Micheline, you will know the affections of L'Ouverture's greatest son."

In Lionel's bed, Micheline fell deeper in love than she thought possible. Lionel knelt between her thighs, gently massaging her knees. He smiled luminously, casting a bright shaft of light across her body. Micheline reached for Lionel, her hands thrumming as she felt his skin. When he was inside her, she thought her heart might stop it seized so painfully. He whispered in her ear, his breath so hot it blistered her. He said, "Everything on this island is mine. You are mine." Micheline moaned. She said, "I am your victory." He said, "Yes, tonight you are." As he fucked her, Micheline heard the bass of a deep drum.

The following morning, Lionel walked Micheline home. He kissed her chastely on the cheek. As he pulled away, Micheline grabbed his hand in hers, pressing a knuckle with her thumb. She said, "I will come to you tonight." Lionel placed one finger over her lips and shook his head. "My dear, we have already had our night."

Micheline was unable to rise from her bed for a long while. She could only remember Lionel's touch, his words, how the inside of her body had molded itself to him. Her parents sent for a doctor, then a priest, and finally a mambo which they were hesitant to do because they were a good, Catholic family but the sight of their youngest daughter lying in bed, perfectly still, not speaking, not eating, was too much to bear. The mambo sat on the edge of the bed and clucked. She held Micheline's limp wrist. She said, "Love," and Micheline nodded. The mambo shooed the girl's parents out of the room and they left, overjoyed that the child had finally moved. The mambo leaned down, got so close. Micheline could feel the old woman's dry lips against her ear.

When the mambo left, Micheline bathed, dabbed herself everywhere she wanted to feel Lionel's lips. She went to Oasis and found Lionel at the center of the room holding a pale, young thing in his lap. Micheline pushed the girl out of Lionel's lap and took her place. She said, "We have had our night but we deserve one more," and Lionel remembered her exquisite moans and the strength of her thighs and how she looked at him like the conquering hero he knew himself to be.

They made love that night, and Micheline was possessed. She dug her fingernails into his back until he bled. She locked her ankles in the small of Lionel's back, and sank her teeth into his strong shoulder. There were no sweet words between them. Micheline walked herself home before he woke. She went to the kitchen and filled a mortar and pestle with blood from beneath her fingernails and between her teeth. She added a few strands of Lionel's hair and a powder the mambo had given her. She ground these things together and put the coup de poudre as it was called into a silk sachet. She ran back to Lionel's, where he was still sleeping, opened her sachet, paused. She traced the edge of his face, kissed his forehead, then blew her precious powder into his face. Lionel coughed in his sleep, then stilled. Micheline undressed and stretched herself along his body, sliding her arm beneath his. As his body grew cooler, she kissed the back of his neck.

They slept entwined for three days. Lionel's skin grew clammy and gray. His eyes hollowed. He began to smell like soil and salt wind. When Micheline woke, she whispered, "Turn and look at me." Lionel slowly turned and stared at Micheline, his eyes wide open, unblinking. She gasped at his appearance, how his body had changed. She said, "Touch me," and Lionel reached for her with a heavy hand, pawing at her until she said, "Touch me gently." She said, "Sit up."

Lionel slowly sat up, listing from side to side until Micheline steadied him. She kissed Lionel's thinned lips, his fingertips. His cold body filled her with a sadness she could hardly bear. She said, "Smile," and his lips stretched tightly into something that resembled what she knew of a smile. Micheline thought about the second silk sachet, the one hidden beneath her pillow between the pages of her Bible, the sachet with a powder containing the power to make Lionel the man he once was—tall, vibrant, the greatest son of L'Ouverture, a man who filled the air with the bass of a deep drum when he walked. She made herself forget about that power; instead, she would always remember that man. She pressed her hand against the sharpness of Lionel's cheekbone. She said, "Love me."

# Sweet on
# the Tongue

M y grandmother, eighty-seven, has changed the name of the nurse's aide who tends to her. She didn't like the woman's real name, said it tasted strange in her mouth. She calls the aide Maria so now we all call the nurse's aide Maria, too. Maria tells me this story when I meet her while visiting my grandmother, who lives with my aunt, next door to another aunt and down the street from more aunts and a few uncles. When we meet, I tell her I already know everything there is to know about her. Information travels at alarming speed through the intricate gossip network of our family. She says, "I could say the same." The way she looks at me makes me uncomfortable. She looks at me the way a man might.

I'm visiting because my grandmother told my mother she didn't want to die without seeing her youngest granddaughter one last time. She makes such pronouncements with regularity. She has been dying for nearly twenty years but no one lives forever.

Maria has a big ass. My grandmother tells Maria this regularly. She has reached that age where she lacks tact. Despite my grandmother's concern about the size of Maria's ass and her unwillingness to call Maria by her given name, they get along quite well. Maria treats my grandmother like her own. She brushes my grandmother's thin, silver hair each night before bed. They love to argue about the shows they watch. They talk about the islands where they were born, the warmth of suns they once knew.

On the first night, my grandmother falls asleep watching the evening news. News of war exhausts her. Maria and I smoke in the small backyard, leaning against a brick wall. My grandmother was not incorrect in her evaluation of Maria's ass but Maria is attractive, not much older than me, dark brown skin, white teeth, soft sweet-smelling skin.

I ask for her real name and she waves a hand limply. "Just call me Maria."

Her accent is familiar. The evening is cold, a cold to which our island skin is not accustomed; it hurts to breathe too deeply. When Maria exhales, I inhale.

"Do you like this kind of work?" I ask.

Maria shrugs, ashes her cigarette. I can no longer see the edges of her face. She steps closer, leans in until I can feel her breasts against mine. "Do you like your kind of work?"

My checks warm.

We fall into a routine over the next several days. When Maria is ready to smoke, she taps my shoulder, lets her fingers rest too long, and I follow her outside. She asks about my life. I can see my family's fingers on her questions. I am vague in my replies.

On Friday, Maria gathers her things while the night nurse, a far less congenial woman, settles in front of the television next to my aunt who is half asleep, her lower lip hanging wetly. Maria nods toward the front door and I follow. On the stoop she says, "I cook," and I say, "I eat." She presses a tightly folded piece of paper into the palm of my hand.

Maria's address is written in block letters and numbers, even her sixes and nines. When I arrive, my fingertips are numb. Maria has changed from scrubs into a denim skirt and a red silk camisole. I stand awkwardly in the hallway, my hands tucked into my armpits.

"You don't have to feed me. This isn't part of your job."

Maria cocks her head. She walks away and I follow dumbly. The apartment is small but clean. The walls are heavy with pictures, many of them black-and-white. We walk down a long hallway to the kitchen, where the air is thick and hot. My pores open hungrily.

"Can I do anything to help?" Maria arches an eyebrow but shakes her head. She points to an empty chair and I sit, shrugging out of my jacket.

I do not visit my family often. Already I am exhausted—so many of them, so demanding, pulling me into meaty embraces and age-old, petty squabbles. I live in Los Angeles in a large loft apartment with a man, Campbell, who works a great deal. He is an agent. He takes care of a select group of clients, all of them stupidly famous. He makes them a stupid amount of money, so he makes a stupid amount of money. We are married and our marriage is complicated but good, better than good. When he proposed he said he understood me. He said all he would ever ask of me is to love him. I do. I don't do anything in the way of compensated work even though I have several degrees that make my lifestyle seem ridiculous at best. Five days a week, I volunteer at a clinic where the people think me far better than I am. Sometimes, Campbell comes home late and I hand him a gin and tonic. We talk about his day. I ask him if he wants a break, if he wants me to help him shoulder the burden of our life together. He squeezes my shoulder and kisses me and takes a long sip of his drink and kisses me again. He says he wants to take care of me.

I met Campbell in the emergency room. He was harried, typing furiously on his phone while standing next to one of his clients, a tabloid bad boy actor who lay on his side, moaning softly. When the actor rolled onto his back, I could see the large bump on his forehead, and next to it, a deep laceration. He reeked of booze. It had been a long shift, full of crazy. The last thing I wanted to deal with was a drunken actor. You've treated one, you've treated them all. I snapped on a pair of gloves and began examining my patient. He made a lewd comment and I slapped his wrist. Three nurses hovered, tittering nervously. I looked up, glaring, but they couldn't help themselves. I finally had to tell them I didn't need their help and closed the curtain. Campbell looked up. He had gray eyes. I thought, I've never seen a black man with gray eyes before, but then he opened his mouth.

"Look, Doc," he said. "If possible, I'd like you to just patch him up, get some fluids in him, and we'll be on our way. No records, no charts."

My eyes narrowed. "Doc? That's not how hospitals work."

Campbell came around to my side of the bed. He was very tall. He looked down. I held his gaze. He squeezed my arm. "Just play ball, sister. You know how it works in this town."

I pulled my arm free. "I'm not your sister. I'm not from this town. I'm afraid I have no idea how *it* works."

The actor started braying.

Hours later, I was at the nurses' station, paper-work, always so much paperwork. I was tired and ready to go home, ready to change out of my scrubs, ready for a long, hot shower. I felt a tap on my shoulder. I looked up, and saw Campbell staring at me. I stood, ready with sharp words.

He held his hands up. "I come in peace. I offer truce."

I put my hands on my hips. "Your client will be here overnight, at least, but he's off my service. Visiting hours start at ten." I turned to return to my paperwork.

Campbell leaned against the desk, crossing his ankles. "So," he said. "What will it take to see you out of scrubs?"

I didn't look up. "Nothing you could possibly offer."

He exhaled loudly, and started walking away but he muttered something under his breath. It wasn't nice.

"I heard that," I shouted after him.

Weeks later, I was on an overnight shift, two in the morning, quiet, sitting in the residents' lounge. I had forgotten about the bad boy actor and his agent. I studied the container of yogurt in my hand, long expired. I ate it anyway, knowing the worst of what could happen. Campbell entered and I looked up, spoon in my mouth.

"You can't be in here," I said, after I swallowed.

"If I can't see you out of scrubs, I will console myself by seeing you in scrubs."

I tried not to appear flustered. "Your client has long been released. I can't imagine what more I can do for you."

Campbell handed me his card. "You can go out with me."

I held the card up to the light. "Is this supposed to be an incentive?" I tossed the card back toward his chest and he caught it, laughing.

"What is with you?"

"I am a humorless resident who works ninety hours a week."

"What do you do during the other seventy-eight hours of the week?"

"I sleep, alone."

Campbell nodded, rubbing his chin, then sat down on the couch, crossing his long legs. "This presents a challenge. If you work ninety hours a week and sleep for the other seventy-eight, that doesn't leave room for much."

"I'm sorry. I'm not sure what you want. Am I supposed to throw myself at you now?"

He patted the empty space next to him. "That would be a start."

I moved to a chair on the other side of the room. "Let's say I went out with you. You'd wine and dine me, maybe take me to a fancy movie premiere, introduce me to shiny people in magazines. We'd sleep together. I'd be deeply unsatisfied. We might go at it a few times more, and then you'd grow bored because I have a brain. We'd be right back where we started. Let's don't and say we did."

Campbell was leaning forward now, his elbows on his knees. "Your anger is fascinating."

"Why do men always assume women are *angry* when they are honest? I'm not angry."

He stood. "You've given me a lot to think about." He disappeared.

His visits became so frequent they grew into a source of amusement in the ER. My coworkers took bets on how long it would take for me to agree to go out with Campbell. I called him a stalker. He told me I was adorable. I said he was a condescending asshole. He agreed, genially. A month passed. For two days, he didn't show up. I spent my entire shift snapping at the nurses, unable to soothe the line of frustration running through me. The next day, when Campbell did show up, I gave him a colder shoulder than usual.

"You missed me, didn't you?" he asked.

I was in the lounge studying an X-ray, a broken leg I would set shortly. "I have no idea what you're talking about."

He took the X-ray from me. "The nurses tell me you've been very short-tempered since we last saw each other."

"Only a man with your arrogance could think that had anything to do with you."

His smile widened. "So it's true."

I grabbed my X-ray back, and accidentally cut myself on the edge. I winced, jumping around as I sucked on the cut.

"Let me see that, you big baby," Campbell said.

I extended my arm, reluctantly. He held my wrist gently, twisting it from side to side to study my finger. He disappeared for a moment and when he returned, he had a Band-Aid, which he applied. He kissed my fingertip and said, "I was out of town on business, film festival, Utah."

As I studied his handiwork, he said, "You should see me for a follow-up. Dinner. Away from here."

I nodded absently. "Sure."

He pumped his fist over his head and I realized what I had just done. The chief resident won the pool at forty-seven days.

On our first date, we sat in a bistro in downtown LA. I studied Campbell's hairline, graying in that terribly appealing way men enjoy. He is older than me by a decade, was married and divorced by the time we met. He started talking about his marriage. I leaned across the table and pressed two fingers against his lips. "Let's not do that. Let's not sit here and tell each other everything there is to know about who we once loved. I am tired of listening to men talk about their regrets."

Campbell's eyes widened and he burst out laughing. "What the fuck?"

"Do you really want to know about the last man or three I slept with or loved?"

He leaned back, lacing his fingers behind his head. "No," he finally said. "I really don't."

"The night just got way better, didn't it?"

Before he could answer, the waiter interrupted, pen at the ready for our order, and Campbell didn't stop staring at me as he told the waiter he wanted the clams.

After a lazy meal and a movie, he walked me to my door and stood real close. "I must admit you've thrown me off my game."

"Good," I said. I leaned in and bit his lower lip then let myself into my house. I had not realized we were holding hands.

On our second date Campbell told me he had someone he wanted me to meet. We pulled up to The Palm and the valet greeted Campbell by name, said his usual table was ready. As Campbell held the door for me, he brushed his hand against the small of my back. We were escorted to a table at the center of the room—a room filled with the thin, beautiful people who typically populate Los Angeles. Some were more recognizable than others. Many of the women shared the same face. At our table, a gorgeous woman was already seated. As I sank into my chair, I recognized her as a movie star having a very good year or at least that's what *People* told me. During lulls in the hospital, I often sat in the waiting room reading the magazines abandoned there. It was the only way I knew anything about anything. She extended a long, willowy arm.

"Your hands are ridiculously soft," I said.

She grinned. "The blood of virgins is the best moisturizer."

I pretended to make a note on the tablecloth. "I will keep that in mind."

Campbell cleared his throat. "Therese, this is Melinda, a dear friend and client. Melinda, Therese. A new friend but not a client."

We nodded and I buried my head in the menu, a large, leather affair. Campbell looked at me over the top of his menu. "Everything is good here."

"If I ate meat, I'm sure it would be."

He looked so uncomfortable, I almost felt sorry for him.

"Dear God. You're a vegetarian."

"If you had been paying attention, you might know that."

His voice lowered. "I am paying attention."

Suddenly his phone rang. He raised a finger in the air, and stepped away from the table to answer the call.

Melinda set her menu down. "He wasn't kidding. You are different."

"Some say."

"You know he invited me here to impress you."

I nodded.

"Is it working?"

"Not even a little."

A waiter delivered a bottle of chilled champagne to the table. After he poured, Melinda and I raised our glasses and smiled.

Maria says everyone is so proud to have a doctor in the family as she sets a plate in front of me—chicken in sauce, rice and peas. I don't tell her I'm a vegetarian.

The skin of the meat glistens. I swallow my nausea and pull my hair into a ponytail.

We are silent as we eat. The meat is salty and tender, breaking apart against my teeth. When we finish, I take the plates to the sink, wash them.

"I volunteer instead of working at a practice or hospital," I say.

Maria laughs. "A doctor is a doctor is a doctor."

We take a bottle of Merlot into the living room. The more wine we drink, the more her accent thickens. Mine does, too.

"Why did you become a doctor?" she asks.

When you're willing to give over so much of your life to a single, impossible pursuit, the questions are inevitable. I tell Maria the truth.

We sit so close our thighs touch. I am dizzy, my mouth empty but full.

"Your grandmother says you haven't been home since . . ."

I shake my head. "Don't."

Maria sighs. "It must have been horrible."

I twist my wedding rings back and forth and think about my husband, how when we're sitting together, he doesn't force me to talk. I worry I am too quiet for him. He says I speak when I need. I speak when it matters.

"Your family wishes you would talk," Maria says.

I pour myself another glass of wine, drink it quickly, and refill my glass again. "I'm sure they talk enough without me. Is this why you asked me here?"

Maria shakes her head, her lips turning down slightly, but I am not convinced. "I do not mean to upset you. I just wanted you to know I know."

I laugh coarsely, and tip my wineglass toward her. "What do you think you know?"

Home is an island in the Caribbean. Some call it a jewel. Everyone who leaves the place calls it home though few of us actually want to be there, not the way it is now. I used to return regularly, often with my mother, holding her hand as the plane descended from the clouds so fast it felt like we would fall into the blue salt of the water. A narrow curve of land would suddenly appear, and the plane would reach for the ground as everyone breathed a sigh of relief.

My father never left the island. He says it is too much to ask a man to leave the only home he has ever known. My parents see each other when they want. They are still married though my father also has a young girlfriend, Roseline, with whom he has two young boys who call my mother and their mother *mama*. Somehow, it works. My mother has a boyfriend too, but he is age appropriate. My father owns a small architecture firm, does reasonably well for himself. As a father, he does reasonably well by his children. We are close.

Maria opens another bottle of wine.

"Why did you leave your island?" I ask. People who leave islands always bring a complex mythology.

She smiles. "Why does anyone leave such places?"

Her manner is infuriating. I look at the clock on the cable box, the green numbers blinking steadily. "I should go."

Maria touches my thigh. "You should stay."

My husband and I married beneath a gauzy canopy on the beach in my country. He wore a tan linen suit with a pink tie. His face was flushed, sweat trembling along his hairline as he tried to adjust to the island heat. The bride wore white, a long, sleeveless dress.

My feet were bare, much to my mother's chagrin. The air was thick with salt and the sand burned beneath our feet. We held hands and stared at each other as we exchanged our vows. He surprised me by saying his vows in my mother tongue, his mouth trying so hard to make those words right. Though I swore I wouldn't, I cried, and smiled so hard my face ached for days. That night, I would carefully massage Caladryl into the skin of his face and whisper sweetly to him. Melinda sat in the front row with her costar from the movie she was filming. Thickly muscled men in dark suits quietly patrolled the beach to keep the paparazzi away. At the reception, his family sat quietly at our table until my father pulled his mother onto the dance floor, and soon all of his relations were drinking rum and waving their hands in the air as they rocked their hips.

Melinda and I stole away for a private moment. We sat near the water's edge, waves lapping our toes. We shared a cigarette.

"I can't believe he won you over." She leaned into me, bumping me with her shoulder.

"He's quite bearable once he stops being Mr. Hollywood."

Melinda sighed. "How did you manage that?" She waved tiredly toward the reception. "I keep dating men who can never turn that off."

I took a long drag. "I made it quite clear from the start that I wasn't remotely interested in where he could take me or who he knows. Once that was settled, he was very easy to love."

She began to move damp sand into a small pile. When she was done, she pulled her knees to her chest, resting her cheek against her legs. "Don't let each other go," she said.

We honeymooned on a private island off the coast. There were no televisions, few tourists, lots of time for stretching our bodies in the sun and getting browner and drinking too much and eating too much. I told him if I found his cell phone, which is one of his vital organs, I would jump up and down on it. He believed me. I'm small but I have big feet. He made me a small boat out of palm fronds and a pointed hat I wore to dinner. We sucked on sugarcane until the insides of our mouths shriveled. I buried him in the hot sand and teased him by lying atop the mound of his body, flicking my tongue against his ear.

Fabien, one of the boys who worked at the resort, took a fancy to me. Campbell pretended to be jealous as Fabien followed me around. When my husband looked away, Fabien flirted aggressively, leaning into me with his shoulders, dancing his fingertips along my arm. He seemed harmless. He had bright, shining eyes. Campbell and I laughed about it when I told him.

One night, Campbell lay across the bed, his lips slick with rum. We wanted to cool our drinks and our skin so I grabbed the ice bucket and walked to the main building. My body hummed with joy. On my way back, Fabien grabbed me by the waist, tried to dance with me. Ice cubes spilled onto the warm pavement. "What are you doing with the *American*?" he asked. His hand slid down to my ass and he squeezed, pressing himself against me. His chest was a flat, hard stretch of muscle. I smiled, and twisted away. I tried to laugh. I said, "No, no, no, I'm a married woman but you are very kind." He tried to kiss me; his lips were salty and thin. I shrieked and bit his lower lip, hard. He cursed, scooping a fallen ice cube from the ground and holding it to his bloody lip. I ran back to our cottage, clutching the ice bucket to my chest. Campbell looked up as I came into the room and slammed the door behind me. My hands shook as I locked the door and set the ice on the dresser and crawled into bed next to him. He asked what took me so long. I stared up at the ceiling fan.

"You're a beautiful woman," says Maria.

Her words are slower now. My mind is slower now. My aunt must be wondering where I am. In the morning, she will nag me incessantly about where I was, what I was doing.

Maria traces my shoulder with one finger. I don't pull away. "You are a mystery to your family," she says. "I feel like I know you."

She presses her lips to the bone of my chin.

This time I pull away. "I am a married woman."

Maria takes a long sip of wine, her teeth clinking against the glass. "I have a husband back home. I hardly remember his face." She sighs. "It is lonely here."

I ignore the tightening in my chest. "It is lonely everywhere."

Maria kisses a gentle line from my forehead to my ear. I stand and go to the window, smeared with a thin layer of grease and fingerprints. I have no idea what is happening. I don't understand my role in it. Down on the street, a young couple argues, the man pacing back and forth along the length of a bus bench while the woman sits on the back of the bench, her feet tapping against the seat.

I press two fingers against the windowpane. "I suppose we both think we know each other," I say.

For the rest of our honeymoon, Fabien lurked. His smile was colder, his eyes not so bright. Campbell and I went back to the mainland and rejoined my parents. We sat in the courtyard of my father's house and told them we had a lovely honeymoon. Heat rose up my neck and through my face as I thought of how night after night, our naked bodies pressed together frantically beneath the mosquito netting, how my husband made me wild for him. Sitting with my parents, Campbell reached for my hand. I laced my fingers through his.

There was a popular market at the center of the capital. On our last day, my husband wanted to see this market. He wanted to be *among my new people*. I rolled my eyes but indulged him. The sun was high, the air so thick we had to push it out of the way to take a step forward. We walked slowly, sweat beading along the edges of our faces, our clothes clinging damply. My husband bought me an ice flavored with grenadine and oranges. I threw bits of ice at his neck. When we came upon a stall of pirated DVDs, he became absorbed. I grew bored. I pressed my hand into the small of his back and said I was going to keep walking. Every few minutes, I turned back to find him and he waved his arm high above his head, grinning. The last time I turned back, he held a stack of movies in his hand, gave me a thumbs-up.

A new swarm of people started milling between us, their bodies making the distance seem impossible. I continued walking, idly touching woven rugs and boxes of Corn Flakes and Levi's jeans. I did not see the man who grabbed me, but at the end of the row of stalls I saw Fabien standing square, staring right at me, his lips curled into a small smile. Before I could make a sound, the man covered my mouth with a hand so large, it practically covered the whole of my face. I had no idea what was happening. I did not understand my place in that moment. I kicked, tried to scratch my way free, but there was little I could do. People saw me being taken. Some shook their heads, offered their pity. Most looked away. I did not see my husband until three days later.

*    *    *

We decided to have the wedding on my island because
a reporter on CNN said the country was safer now,
said the beaches were once again full of pale American tourists, Canadians, too. The troubles, the reporter
said, would soon be a distant memory. We believed
him because I thought it would be wonderful to marry
the man I loved on the soil of the country I loved before
I learned how to love anything else.

I was returned to my family in the early morning,
when the air was almost cool and the sky was dark gray
like Campbell's eyes. I sat in the back of a pickup truck,
holding on to the rusted edge as the broken roads
tossed me from side to side. My kidnappers didn't say
a word as they lifted me out of the truck bed and set
me on the ground. With a light shove, they pushed me
toward my father's house and drove off, gravel spitting
from their tires. I shivered as I knocked softly. I waited.
In the distance, a rooster crowed mournfully. When no
one answered, I knocked harder, wincing because my
knuckles were tender. Finally, my husband answered,
his eyes widening. He spread his arms open as he said,
"Oh my God." I planted my hand against his chest and

pushed him away. I refused to look in his face and slid past him, locked myself in our room. I leaned against the door as he knocked. He was soon joined by my parents, the three of them pounding their fists against the door, trying to break it down to reach me, pleading for me to let them in.

"Please be quiet," I said. "I need to think. Please let me think." When I was ready, I took a deep breath and opened the door.

They spoke fast. I couldn't hold on to their words.

"Nothing happened. A group of men grabbed me from the market and took me to a sugar warehouse on the edge of the city. They left me alone." I looked at Campbell. "When you paid the ransom, they brought me here."

My husband shook his head, slowly. "Baby," he said. "Baby." He clasped my shoulder gently and turned me toward a full-length mirror on the wall.

I did not know who I was looking at. The woman in the mirror, her face swelled with dark bruises. The corner of her lip was split and angry. Her tank top was torn along the waist in several places. Her jeans were soiled.

I shook my head. "Nothing happened."

*       *       *

Maria joins me at the window. "It is so strange," she says, "living in a place with so much steel and concrete. All these buildings, they don't even seem real."

I shrug. "Do you have children?" I ask, turning around.

Maria shakes her head and returns to the couch, the cushion beneath her sighing. "Not yet."

I hold my hand against my chest and swallow. "I have a son. He is three."

Maria coughs. "Your family did not mention you have a child."

"Haven't you learned, Maria? My family doesn't know anything about me."

The captain of the local precinct came to the house immediately. I told him I had no information to help him find my kidnappers. He appeared grateful but spoke of an investigation that would be ongoing, how justice would be served. He drank my father's coffee and ate sweet cake, his shoulders slumped. There was nothing he could do no matter what I told him, no matter what he said. I excused myself as my parents and husband and the captain spoke and made empty statements about the cruelty of the world. I locked myself in the bathroom, filled the tub with hot water, and sank into it, watching as the water turned pink, the dried blood on my body dissolving slowly. I closed my eyes and sank beneath the surface. The rush of heavy silence overwhelmed me until it comforted me. When Campbell found me, I was sitting on our bed, drying my hair with a towel.

"You need to see a doctor," he said, sitting next to me.

I slid away but I didn't mean to. I said, "I am a doctor."

Later that afternoon, we were on a charter flight to Manhattan where a friend of mine from medical school had privileges at Beth Israel. The plane was well appointed—leather seats, lacquered surfaces, and alcohol I drank, liberally. My skin and muscle and bone hurt. We were silent for a long while. I did not look out the window.

Finally, I cleared my throat. "It shouldn't be too difficult to get an annulment."

Campbell's face rearranged into a hard line. "What the hell are you talking about?" He slammed his fist against the wall. "What the hell are you talking about?"

It was the first and only time he has raised his voice to me. His anger filled the cabin until there was no air. A loud ringing made my ears ache. I started shaking.

He covered my hand with his. "You are my wife," he said. "You are safe with me."

I closed my eyes and opened them again.

When I was working crazy shifts during my residency, Campbell brought me coffee, hot food, his smile. We went up to the roof and sat on a pair of lawn chairs. We'd hold hands. Many times, he pushed me to the ground, pulling my scrubs down around my ankles, taking me as I stared into the starry night sky and held on to him as tightly as I could. He whispered, "I love you so much" into the skin of my neck as I rose to meet him.

On the plane that day, I said, "I can't breathe. I can't do anything." I leaned against him, pressing my forehead against the strength of his arm. I held his wrists so he wouldn't wrap his arms around me. He whispered into the skin of my neck.

Maria and I open yet another bottle of wine. I don't remember the last time I drank this much. Or I do. My body feels loose, like every part of me is falling away.

"My son is very smart," I say. "Only three years old and he knows so much. I saw it in his eyes from the day he was born that he would know lots of important things." I cross my legs, bouncing my foot. "He has a sweet tooth, just like my grandmother. If you give him candy, he will love you all his life. He is perfect."

Maria nods and smiles. "Why didn't you bring him?" She is skeptical.

I study the painting on the wall above the television—geometric shapes in metallic colors surrounding a woman carrying a woven basket on her head. "That isn't possible. Is it hard to be away from your husband?"

Maria slides a hand between my thighs. She kisses my shoulder and my neck and my cheek and brushes her lips across mine. "I find ways to keep from being terribly lonely."

I sit perfectly still.

When we arrived at the hospital, my friend Natalya was waiting at the entrance. I held on to my husband's arm and walked slowly. She ushered us into an examination room. I stood in the corner. Campbell tried to sit down. I looked at Natalya and shook my head.

She smiled, told him he should go to the waiting room.

"I'm not leaving you," he said.

I held on to the wall to steady myself. "I don't want you to see me differently."

He closed his fingers into tight fists. "That could never happen." My knees were on the verge of buckling. He reached for me. "You're shaking," Campbell said.

I tried to back away. "Don't touch me." I was hysterical, barely coherent.

My husband paled. "You're afraid of me."

Natalya gently took hold of his elbow and pulled him out of the room. I wanted to call out to him but my throat locked. I was mute.

Later he would tell me he waited just outside the door the entire time. I would have known even if he hadn't told me.

Natalya returned. "Alone at last," she said. She's the amiable sort, the one everyone got along with, even the med students with claws. "You came to the right person. You're going to get through this."

I half laughed then covered my mouth to catch an ugly sob. My face was wet, my lips salty. Natalya wrapped her arms around me and smoothed my hair over and over. She said, "Shhh." I allowed myself to fall into her.

Later, after the examination; after the revolting terror of my body revealing the truth of what happened; after needles in my arm taking my blood from me; after large pills I struggled to swallow down my raw, aching throat; after stitches on my face, my chest, in places I did not know could be stitched; after my wrist, X-rays of which revealed fractures in sharp relief, was splinted and wrapped in a cast, Natalya said, "I am not going to say anything but I'm sorry this happened to you and you can talk to me if you want, need, anything you need."

I wanted to tell her, to tell anyone, but the words thickened on my tongue and stayed there, rotting slowly.

Maria slides her hand beneath my shirt, pressing the palm of her hand against my navel. Her hand is surprisingly cool. I exhale slowly. She slides her hand higher. Just before she cups my breast, I grab her wrist and push her hand away. "I am happily married," I say.

Maria nips the fleshy part of my earlobe. "As am I."

This time I push her away roughly, stand, and look for my jacket. "You have no right."

"I would have thought you might appreciate the touch of a woman after everything."

"You don't know anything about me. Nothing happened."

"I understand why that version of the truth suits you."

A hot rush of anger suddenly fills my mouth. I pull Maria up from the couch, and force her hand to my crotch. "Is this what you want?"

"You're family is right. You are a very cold woman," Maria says.

"Only to people who don't know me."

We did not stay in New York long. I wanted to go home. Melinda was waiting in our loft. I hadn't spoken since the hospital. Campbell was out of his mind, trying to fix me.

Melinda gasped when she saw me, stood, and held her hands open. "I do not know what to say."

My face was frozen, muscles locked. I couldn't look her in the eye.

"She hasn't spoken in two days," Campbell said.

I walked past them to the balcony and stood alone, in the waning light.

When Melinda joined me, I refused to turn around. I studied the scenery below and took long drags on my cigarette.

When our eyes finally met, all she could say was, "Oh honey."

I didn't make sense of it at first. I couldn't keep food down. I assumed my body was trying to recover. Four months after our honeymoon, the last of the bruises finally faded, I was back at work. Campbell made me pancakes on a Saturday morning while I sat quietly on the kitchen counter. I asked for one and he handed it to me on the spatula. I grinned as I pulled the warm pancake apart. He smiled back. I reached for him with my feet and pulled him between my legs. I fed him bits of pancake. I let him hold me for the first time since our honeymoon. "Look at you," Campbell whispered into my neck. I kissed his stubbled chin, his lips, shyly at first and then not so shyly. My mouth and my body remembered him. He groaned, pulling at my clothes and I let him but then my stomach rolled uncomfortably. I had to push him away.

I ran to the bathroom and as I heaved into the toilet, I knew and it was the worst kind of knowing. I had taken the pills. This wasn't supposed to happen. I pounded my fists against the toilet seat.

Campbell stood over me, worried. I couldn't look at him. "I need a pregnancy test."

I looked up and saw how his features brightened, a wide smile stretching across his face. And then his smile became something else. I went to our room and changed. I left. I ignored my phone until the battery died. When it grew dark, I pulled into a Walmart parking lot and made sure my doors were locked. I tried to sleep. I wanted to quiet the screaming in my head.

In the morning, the screaming was louder, sharper, more singular. My head throbbed. I walked into the Walmart, bought a test, and went into the bathroom, where it was humid and dirty. I squatted in the last stall and held the stick between my thighs. I gritted my teeth and pissed. I didn't need to look at the readout to know it would read *Yes*.

I find my coat and thank Maria for the dinner. It has been a long, strange evening. She is nervous as she unlocks her front door. "Please don't tell your family about this."

I brush my fingers across her knuckles. "I don't tell my family anything."

It is much colder outside but I walk slowly. The streets are empty which scares me. In the four years since our honeymoon, I have always been scared. I have felt a spiraling terror lodged in my throat. I have tried to cut that terror out.

I found my husband sitting in the hall entrance of our loft. He hadn't shaved. His eyes were wild with anger and something else. He looked up at me and when he spoke his voice was uncomfortably calm. "After what happened, I would think you would be considerate enough to call if you aren't coming home."

I stepped toward him then stopped. "I didn't realize," I said. "I didn't think."

"Your pancakes are cold."

I handed him the pregnancy test. "It could be yours."

He patted the floor next to him and I slowly lowered myself to the floor. "Tell me what happened. If I know, I can help you. I can try."

"Do you want to know or do you need to know?"

Campbell cracked his knuckles. "I want. Because it's what's best for you."

Once again, my throat locked. I shook my head.

I sit on the cold concrete steps of my aunt's stoop and call Campbell. I am very drunk.

"Can you come out here?" I ask, my words slurring.

"What's wrong?" His voice is dry and hoarse.

"I have a son, Campbell." It feels good to release those words from my chest again.

"Yes, we do."

"That is the perfect thing to say."

"It's the truth."

"I had too much to drink and a woman hit on me and tried to kiss me. It was weird."

"And I didn't get to watch?" His voice is clearer now.

I laugh. "You're a pig."

"Are you okay? Did you kiss her back?"

"Yes. A little, no tongue. I really drank a lot."

"You are so LA now."

"I miss our son every time I breathe. I miss you."

I can hear Campbell moving now.

"I'm ready to make another baby."

I close my eyes. The phone grows warmer against my cheek.

"Are you there? I didn't mean anything by that."

"I'm ready, too," I say, softly.

The paternity test confirmed my worst fears. I couldn't get rid of it, old country ways, and knew I couldn't keep it. It was easy to find a family looking for a baby. I started to show so I quit my job at the hospital even though I had just finished my residency. It would have been too much to explain why Campbell and I, who did want children, couldn't keep this child, to answer questions, to pretend to be joyful, to talk about a life I would never know. I hid in our loft. Campbell brought me screeners. I realized movies had gotten much worse since I started medical school.

When she was in town, Melinda spent hours with me, trying to get me to talk, regaling me with stories of this or that event, the latest gossip from the set of her film and how things were going with her costar, a man she described as violently committed to dullness. My stomach swelled. The baby was active, always swimming around, kicking me, tearing my heart apart. Early on I told Campbell I would move out until the baby was born. He did not appreciate the gesture, refused. He tried to reach me but I kept him out. We were living together but we weren't. I refused to look at myself in mirrors. My body was the worst kind of prison, utterly inescapable. One day, toward the end, Campbell found me in the study, holding my belly, talking softly. It was the first time I really touched the baby.

"Look at you," he said. "You're beautiful."

I quickly let my arms fall to the side. "This doesn't mean anything." I shuffled out of the room as quickly as I could, leaving him stammering in my wake.

Melinda is the only person I allowed in the delivery room. Campbell was furious but I told him I wanted him in the delivery room when I gave birth to our child. I wanted to save that moment for him. My best friend held my hand and pressed cold cloths to my forehead. She didn't fill the air with useless chatter.

There are no words to describe how it feels to push a baby out of your body. Before the kidnapping, I would have thought it was the most inconceivable pain a woman can experience but I knew better. When you give birth, you willingly break yourself. You allow your body to come apart. Each time I pushed, even though I was so miserable and exhausted, I held on to the promise of soon being free. I needed to rid myself of the terrible thing inside me.

The nurse who laid the slick, squealing child on my chest didn't realize I had written in my birth plan that I didn't want to look upon him. I forced myself to look at him. His head was covered with a sticky matte of dark hair. His arms were so skinny but his hands were what splintered the hard shell around me, so tiny, fingers splayed as he reached for my face. I cupped his tiny head and kissed his forehead. He quieted, his lips quivering. I wanted to pull him into my rib cage and hold him inside my body once more. I was staggered by him, my beautiful boy.

"I need time with him," I whispered, to no one in particular. I prayed they would grant me this one wish.

Everyone in the room exchanged looks, but after the baby was cleaned and swaddled, he was placed in my arms once more. He stared at me with wide eyes. I kissed his cheeks, soft and the warmest shade of brown with a hint of red. "I didn't know," I said, holding him as tightly as I dared. "I didn't know I would love you." I saw nothing of his father in the boy, not one single thing. It was a mercy.

Melinda slipped out of the room. When the door opened again, it was Campbell, who ran to my side. He looked at the baby, his eyes watery and wide open. He covered my hand with his.

"I don't think I can let him go," I said, my voice cracking. "I'm sorry. I did not expect this. I didn't know. I don't know what to do." I started to cry and then I was sobbing from somewhere deep, sobbing for the woman who had spent the past nine months on a sticky floor in a hot sugar warehouse with strange, violent men.

Campbell pushed the railing down and climbed into bed with me. His shoes fell loudly to the floor as he kicked them off. He wiped my tears as quickly as they fell. "You don't have to let him go," he said.

I brushed my fingers across the baby's forehead. "I didn't know."

The baby yawned and closed his eyes. I couldn't keep my eyes open.

It was dark outside when I awoke. I was alone in my hospital room. I remembered the soft, warm weight of the baby against my chest. The absence was unbearable. I panicked, shot up, then winced. I pressed the call button and a few minutes later, a tired-looking nurse padded into my room. "My baby," I croaked. "Did they take him? Is it too late?"

The nurse smiled. "He's in the nursery. His father is with him—wanted you to get some rest. They'll be back soon. New mothers can sleep with their babies if they want."

The tight pain in my chest slowly began to unravel. "I want," I said.

I sat up and stared at the door, the waiting interminable. When he returned, Campbell was pushing a bassinet, the baby swaddled in a blue blanket, wearing a little blue hat, fast asleep.

"He was fussy," Campbell said, "We went to the nursery to hang out." He waved his wrist, showing off a hospital bracelet matching the baby's and mine. "They gave me one of these. I got to feed him with a tiny bottle the size of two of my fingers." My husband looked different, softer. His face couldn't contain his smile. He was giddy.

"What about . . . ?"

"I notified the lawyer. They're disappointed, of course, but this was always a possibility. People in their situation know that."

"I have done a terrible thing."

"No, you haven't. I explained what I could." He pressed his fingers against the baby's forehead. "I know people," he said. "I'm going to do everything in my power to help them."

The baby shifted slightly and made an adorable, wet sound.

"We're not ready for this. We have no idea what we're doing. We don't even have a car seat. We drive ridiculous cars. I'm sorry. You didn't sign up for this."

"Stop apologizing. This is exactly what I signed up for."

I began fiddling with my hospital bracelet. "You don't know."

"I want you to tell me."

I pointed to the baby. "He can never know, Campbell. Never. Do you understand?"

My husband nodded.

I carefully got out of bed and went to the window. A dull ache throbbed between my thighs.

"Don't look away," Campbell said.

I ignored him. "I thought I would never be able to love him right. I thought he would always be a reminder. I will never know who made him. I don't want to."

\*    \*    \*

I was taken to a sugar warehouse and thrown into a room with no furniture, the floor sticky with sweet grime. I couldn't think. I was terrified. It was unspeakably hot. I could hardly breathe. Hours later, a fat man with a shiny, bald, head appeared. He said the wife of a rich American was worth a lot of money. He told me to undress. I didn't know what to do. The man backhanded me. I looked into his eyes to try and make sense of the kind of man he was. I took too long. He backhanded me again and drove his fist into my stomach. My gut wrenched. I told him my husband would pay for me. He tore my clothes from my body and dragged me by my hair into a large room filled with a mountain of raw sugar that reached to the ceiling. He threw me down and the sugar scratched my bare skin. He unbuckled his pants. I begged. There was nowhere to run, men everywhere.

He climbed on top of me, so heavy. I have never stopped feeling his wet skin against mine. Our bodies sank into that mountain of sugar. Grains of sugar floated in the air as he thrust. In the shafts of sunlight filling the warehouse, the sugar looked beautiful so that's what I looked at. I couldn't close my eyes no matter how hard I tried. Grains of sugar fell on my tongue as I screamed. The sugar beneath me hardened with my blood. And then there was another man and another and another, each crueler. When it was over, I balled myself into a corner to wait. By the end, I was wild and vicious, scratching and clawing at anything that came near me. After, they drove me to my father's house. Fabien sat in the back of the truck with me. He said, "If only you had given me a little kiss," smiling like a spurned child. He tried to kiss me, fumbling at my body with his foolish hands. I snapped, screaming hoarsely as I clawed at his face, felt his skin come away. They had to stop the truck to pull us apart. As he got into the cab, he cursed me. I looked at my hands, red and raw, holding a piece of his skin. I slapped it against the cab window. He held his face as he turned around to stare at me. I never looked away.

When I finished speaking, I turned back to Campbell. "I did not want to look at my child and be forced to remember that. I did not want to love him less than he deserved. I did not want to hate him, which he did not deserve."

Campbell knelt by the side of the bed. He took my hands, kissing them over and over. He didn't say anything useless. He didn't try to change what could not be changed.

Campbell flies out to meet me. I wait on the sidewalk as a town car pulls up. Campbell Jr., C.J., bounds out of the car first, his arms thrust high in the air. I still don't see the men who forced their way into me when I look at my son. I hope I never will. C.J. jumps into my arms and I clasp the back of his head. The curved bone fits perfectly in my palm. I can breathe again. I cover his face in kisses and he giggles. He says, "Mommy, mommy, mommy." Campbell tips the driver. I grab his shirt and pull him in. When he kisses me, I am home.

"I never thought this day would come," Campbell says.

I slide my hand into the pocket of his jeans, pulling him closer still. "I am ready."

Maria is startled when we walk into my aunt's house. "You have a son," she says, stuttering.

Campbell is holding him now, our son drowsy from the long flight, his arms hanging limply at his sides.

"I told you I did."

She clears her throat. I don't know what she wants from me, who she wants me to be. She studies Campbell. In my mother tongue, she says, "You married an old man." I want to claw her eyes out. I hold Campbell's arm possessively. Finally, she says, "I must attend to your grandmother."

As she walks away, Campbell elbows me. "I'm not that old. She has a big ass."

That evening, I sit with my grandmother, holding C.J. in my lap, surrounded by the smell and joy of him.

"Such a beautiful boy," she says. Her eyes are milky. I hold her hand, can feel the fragility of that network of bones.

"I wanted you to know him."

C.J. claps his hands and sings a song I don't recognize. He loves to sing. Sometimes, Campbell and I hear him on the baby monitor, singing in his room. We laugh and laugh and laugh.

"Do you want to give your great-grandmother a kiss?" I whisper into C.J.'s ear.

He nods politely, and leans in, leaving a loud, wet kiss on her cheek. He squirms out of my arms and runs away.

"Campbell," I say, loudly. "He's on his way to you."
I hold my breath until I hear Campbell growl and C.J.
growls back—it's this thing they do I don't pretend to
understand. I can still feel my son in the room. Some
part of him is always with me.

My grandmother leans in to me, says my aunt is
stealing her money. I listen carefully. I take her seri-
ously. She's not allowed to have money. She'll use it to
bribe Maria to bring her cakes and other confections.
She has always had a sweet tooth and Maria is cor-
ruptible. My grandmother's tongue, like my son's, is
awfully fond of sugar.

# Cheap, Fast,
Filling

When Lucien arrives in the United States by way of Canada, an illegal but uneventful border crossing, and hitching rides down to Miami, his cousin Christophe, who made his own way to Miami years earlier, hands him a fifty-dollar bill and tells Lucien to eat Hot Pockets until he gets a job because they are cheap, filling, and taste good. Lucien sleeps on the floor in an apartment he shares with five other men like him, all of them pretending this life is better than that which came before. There is a small kitchen with an electric stove that has two burners and a microwave that is rarely cleaned. Christophe tells Lucien that Hot Pockets are easy to prepare.

Lucien is in the United States because he loves *Miami Vice*. He loves the shiny suits Tubbs and Crockett wear. He loves their swagger. He loves the idea of Miami as a perfect place where problems are always solved and there are beautiful women as far as a man can see. In secondaire, Lucien would daydream about Miami while the French nuns frowned and slapped his desk with their rulers. He has not yet seen that Miami but he knows it is there. It has to be.

Lucien's apartment is in Pembroke Pines—a world away from Little Haiti and everything that might be familiar in an unfamiliar place. Every morning, he wakes up at five, showers, gets dressed. He walks four miles to the Home Depot on Pines Boulevard where he waits for contractors to cruise through the parking lot looking for cheap, fast labor. He stands in the immigrant bazaar with the Mexicans and Guatemalans and Nicaraguans, sometimes a few Chinese. They stand tall, try to look strong, hope that a long white finger will curl in their direction. Three or four times a week, he is lucky. He grabs his tool belt, hauls himself into the truck bed, and enjoys the humid morning air as he is driven to big houses owned by white people locked behind gates to keep their things safe from people like him even though he has never stolen a thing in his life.

Once a week, Lucien buys a calling card for twenty-five dollars. It will allow him to talk for twenty-eight minutes. He calls home and talks to his mother, his uncle, his wife, his four children. He tells elaborate fables about his new life—how he's found them a new home with a bedroom for each child, and air-conditioning so they can breathe cool, dry air. There is a lawn with green grass and a swimming pool in the backyard by which his wife can lie in the sun. His children, two boys and two girls all under the age of ten, clamor for his attention. He strains to understand them through the static on the line. They tell him about school and their friends and the UN soldier who is renting a room in the house, how he's teaching them Brazilian curse words. When there are only a few minutes left, his wife chases the children into the bedroom they all share. They are alone. There is no time for anything tender. She whispers that she needs Lucien to send more money, there's no food, there's no water. She wants to know when he will send for them. He lies. He tells her he's doing all he can. He says soon.

On the weekends, Christophe picks Lucien up in the truck his boss lets him take home and they go to house parties in Little Haiti. They listen to konpa and drink rum, as all Haitians are wont to do. They philosophize about how to solve their country's problems.

"Haiti," his father would always tell Lucien while he was growing up, "is a country with seven million dictators." Sometimes, when it is very late at night, Lucien will find comfort in the arms of a woman who is not his wife. He will go home with her and in the darkness, as he cups her breasts with his hands and listens to her breathing against him, as he presses his lips against her neck and her shoulder, then licks the salt from her skin, he will imagine she tastes like home.

Around the corner from Lucien's apartment is a 7-Eleven. Sometimes, when he can't sleep, Lucien likes to go there because it is cool and bright and clean and he can buy Hot Pockets. The man who works there late at night is also Haitian. He understands why Lucien likes to walk slowly up and down each aisle, carefully studying each row filled with perfectly packaged products. When the clerk first arrived in Miami, he did the same thing. Lucien thinks about the sweet things he would buy for his children if they were with him and how much it would please him to watch them eat a Twix or a Kit Kat. Each night, before he leaves 7-Eleven, Lucien buys two Hot Pockets that he microwaves, and a Super Big Gulp. He walks home and sits on the curb in front of his building so he can be alone. He drinks slowly, so slowly there's no ice left in the cup when he's done. He eats one of the Hot Pockets and the other one, he holds. He enjoys its warmth, thinks he's holding the whole of the world in his hands.

# In the Manner
## of Water
## or Light

My mother was conceived in what would ever after be known as the Massacre River. The sharp smell of blood has followed her since. When she first moved to the United States, she read the dictionary from front to back. Her vocabulary quickly became extensive. Her favorite word is suffuse, to spread over or through in the manner of water or light. When she tries to explain how she is haunted by the smell of blood, she says that her senses are suffused with it.

My grandmother knew my grandfather for less than a day.

Everything I know about my family's history, I know in fragments. We are the keepers of secrets. We are secrets ourselves. We try to protect each other from the geography of so much sorrow. I don't know that we succeed.

As a young woman, my grandmother worked on a sugarcane plantation in Dajabón, the first town across the border Haiti shares with the Dominican Republic. She lived in a shanty with five other women, all strangers, and slept on a straw mat beneath which she kept her rosary, a locket holding a picture of her parents, and a picture of Clark Gable. She spoke little Spanish so she kept to herself. Her days were long and beneath the bright sun, her skin burned ebony and her hair bleached white. When she walked back to her quarters at the end of each day, she heard the way people whispered and saw how they stared. They steered clear. They were terrified by the absence of light around and within her. They thought she was a demon. They called her la demonia negra.

After saying her prayers, after dreaming of Port-au-Prince and lazy afternoons at the beach and the movie house where she watched *Mutiny on the Bounty* and *It Happened One Night* and *Call of the Wild*, after dreaming of the warmth of Clark Gable's embrace, my grandmother would tear her old dresses into long strips so she could better bind the cuts and scratches she'd earned from a long day in the cane fields. She would sleep a dreamless sleep, gathering the courage she would need to wake up the next morning. In a different time, she had been loved by two parents, had lived a good life, but then they died and she was left with nothing, and like many Haitians, she crossed over into the Dominican Republic in the hope that there, her luck would change. My grandfather worked at the same plantation. He was a hard worker. He was a tall, strong man. My grandmother, late at night when she cannot sleep, will sit with a glass of rum and Coke, and talk about how her hands remember the thick ropes of muscle in his shoulders and thighs. His name was Jacques Bertrand. He wanted to be in the movies. He had a bright white smile that would have made him a star.

My grandmother is also haunted by smells. She cannot stand the smell of anything sweet. If she smells sweetness in the air, she purses her lip and sucks on her teeth, shaking her head. Today, when we drive to our family's beach property in Montrouis, she closes her eyes. She can stand neither the sight of the cane fields nor that of the withered men and women hacking away at stubborn stalks of cane with dull machetes. When she sees the cane fields, a sharp pain radiates across her shoulders and down her back. Her body cannot forget the labors it has known.

Now, the Massacre River is shallow enough to cross by foot, but in October 1937, the waters of what was the Dajabón River ran strong and deep. The unrest had been going on for days—Dominican soldiers determined to rid their country of the Haitian scourge went from plantation to plantation in a murderous rage. My grandmother did the only thing she could, burning through a long day in the cane field, marking the time by the rise and fall of her machete blade. She prayed the trouble would pass her by.

It was General Rafael Trujillo who ordered all the Haitians out of his country, who had his soldiers interrogate anyone whose skin was too dark, who looked like they belonged on the other side of the border. It was the general who took a page from the Book of Judges to exact his genocide and bring German industry to his island.

Soldiers came to the plantation where my grandmother worked. They had guns. They were cruel; spoke in loud, angry voices; took liberties. One of the women with whom my grandmother shared her shanty betrayed my grandmother's hiding place. We never speak of what happened after that. The ugly details are trapped between the fragments of our family history. We are secrets ourselves.

My grandmother ended up in the river. She found a shallow place. She tried to hold her breath while she hid from the marauding soldiers on both of the muddy shores straddling the river. There was a moment when she lay on her back, and submerged herself until her entire body was covered by water, until her pores were suffused with it. She didn't come up for air until the ringing in her ears became unbearable. The moon was high and the night was cold. She smelled blood in the water. She wore only a thin dress, plastered to her skin. Her feet were bare. When a bloated corpse slowly floated past her, then an arm, a leg, something she couldn't recognize, she covered her mouth with her hand. She screamed into her own skin instead of the emptiness around her.

Jacques Bertrand who worked hard and wanted to be in the movies found his way to the river that ran strong and deep. He moved himself through the water until he found my grandmother. He tapped her on the shoulder and instead of turning away, she turned to him, opened that part of her herself not yet numb with terror. She found comfort in the fear mirrored in his eyes. His chest was bare and she pressed her damp cheek against his breastbone. She slowed her breathing to match his. She listened to the beat of his heart; it echoed beneath the bones of his rib cage. "An angel," she told me. "I thought he was an angel who had come to deliver me from that dark and terrible place."

My grandparents bound their bodies together as their skin gathered in tiny folds, as their bodies shook violently. Jacques Bertrand, who worked hard, who wanted to be in the movies, wrapped his arms around my grandmother. In a stuttered whisper, he told her the story of his life. "I want to be remembered," he said. She cupped his face in her hands, traced his strong chin with her thumbs, and brushed her lips across his. She followed the bridges of scar tissue across his back with her fingertips. She said, "You will be remembered." She told him the story of her own life. She asked him to remember her, too.

My grandmother still hears the dying screams from that night. She remembers the dull, wet sound of machetes hacking through flesh and bone. The only thing that muted those horrors was a man she knew but did not know who wore bridges of scar across his back. I do not know the intimate details, but my mother was conceived.

In the morning, surrounded by the smell and silence of death, my grandparents crawled out of the river that had, overnight, become a watery coffin holding twenty-five thousand bodies. The Massacre River had earned its name. The two of them, soaking wet, their bodies stiff and on the verge of fever, crawled into Ouanaminthe. They were home. They were far from home. My grandmother laced her fingers with my grandfather's and they sought refuge in an abandoned church. They fell to their knees and prayed and then their prayers became something else, something like solace.

When night fell again, the Dominican soldiers crossed into Ouanaminthe, into a place they did not belong. My grandfather was killed. He saved my grandmother's life by confronting three soldiers, creating a window through which my grandmother could escape. Jacques Bertrand died wanting to be remembered, so my grandmother stayed in that place of such sorrow, took a job cooking and cleaning for the headmaster of a primary school. At night, she slept in an empty classroom. She gave birth to my mother and later married the headmaster who raised my mother as his own. At night, my grandmother took my mother to the river and told her the story of how she came to be. My grandmother knelt on the riverbank, her bones sinking in the mud as she brought handfuls of water to her mouth. She drank the memories in that water.

When my mother turned twelve, she, my grandmother, and the headmaster moved to Port-au-Prince. The school had closed and the headmaster took a new appointment in the capital. At first, my grandmother refused to leave her memories, but the headmaster put his foot down. She was his wife. She would follow. My mother recalls how her mother wailed, her voice pitched sharp and thin, cutting everything around her. In the front yard of their modest home, a large coconut tree fell, its wide trunk split neatly in half. The fallen fruit rotted instantly. My grandmother went to the Massacre River, her long white hair gathered around her face. She took river mud into her hands, eating it, enduring the thick, bitter taste. When my mother and the headmaster found her, my grandmother was lying in a shallow place, shivering beneath a high moon, her face caked with dry mud.

In the capital, my grandmother was a different woman, quieted. The headmaster consulted Catholic missionaries, houngans, and mambos in case she had been possessed by an lwa or spirit, and needed healing. Finally, he resigned himself to living with her ghosts. He loved her as best a man whose wife loves another man can. He focused on my mother's education and waited. Sometimes, the headmaster asked my mother if she was happy. She said, "My mother does love you."

It wasn't until the day my mother left Port-au-Prince that my grandmother became herself again. I've been told that the headmaster and my grandmother stood on the tarmac white with heat, the air billowing around them in visible waves. My mother kissed her mother twice on each cheek. She kissed the headmaster. She turned and headed for the staircase to board the plane, a heavy wind blowing her skirt wildly. My grandmother didn't run after her only child but she did say, "Ti Couer." Little heart. My mother stopped. She didn't turn around.

My mother is a small, nervous woman. Her life began, she says, the day she got off the Pan Am flight from Port-au-Prince in New York City. She sat in the back of a yellow taxicab driven by a man who spoke a language she did not understand. She stared out the dirty window and up at the tall steel buildings. She was twenty-one. My mother found an apartment in the Bronx. She took a job as a seamstress for Perry Ellis making clothes she loved but could not afford. She learned to speak English by reading the dictionary and watching American television. Once a month, she wrote her mother and the only father she knew a long letter telling them about America, begging them to join her. My grandmother always wrote back, but refused to leave Haiti. She would not leave the ghost of a man who could not be forgotten.

My mother went to doctor after doctor trying to find someone who would free her from a sharp smell of blood that has always suffused her senses. Each doctor assured my mother it was all in her head. She took the subway to Chinatown and tried acupuncture. The acupuncturist carefully inserted needles into the webs of her thumbs and along her body's meridians. As he placed each needle, he shook his head. He said, "There are some things no medicine can fix."

When I asked my mother how she met my father she said, "I wasn't going to marry a Haitian man." She rarely answers the question she is asked. My father is an ear, nose, and throat specialist. He is the last doctor my mother consulted. When she told him she could only smell blood, he believed her. He tried to help her and when he couldn't, he asked her to join him for dinner. Eventually he asked for her hand in marriage. She didn't say yes. She told my father she would never return to Haiti, that he would have to accept that her life began a year earlier. She was a seamstress whose senses were suffused with the smell of blood, who didn't know her father and couldn't understand her mother. They were married in a Manhattan synagogue, nine months after they met.

My parents remained childless for many years but never discussed the matter. If my mother was asked when she would start a family, she would say, "I am very much in love with my husband." When she learned she was pregnant with me, at the age of forty, it was a hot July afternoon in New York, 1978. She ran out onto to the street, threw her hands in the air, stared into the incandescent sun. She cried as the light spread over her. A joyful sound vibrated from her throat, through her mouth, and into the city around her. She went to my father's office and told him the news. He cried, too. When I was born, I was crying lustily. We are a family unafraid of our tears.

My mother has never been able to accept she will never know her real father. She worries her mother has woven the story of her conception into an elaborate fable to hide a darker truth. My mother has an imagination. She knows too much about what angry, wild soldiers will do to frightened, fleeing young women. My mother looks in the mirror and cannot recognize herself. She sees only the face of a man she can never know. When I was a little girl and we sat together at the dinner table, my mother often stared into the distance, grinding her teeth. My father would take her hand and say, "Jacqueline, please stop worrying." She never did. She was the keeper of her mother's secrets. She was a secret herself.

Every summer, once I turned five, my parents took me to JFK and sent me to my grandmother for three months. I was dispatched to do the work of a dutiful daughter in my mother's absence. My grandmother and the man I know as my grandfather, the headmaster who took in a scared young woman whose skin had burned ebony, whose hair had bleached white, who bore a child with no father, they were kind to me. I brought them pictures of my parents and money my mother carefully stuffed in my shoes. I brought cooking oil and panty hose, a VCR and videotapes, gossip magazines, Corn Flakes. I knew never to bring anything sweet.

My grandmother kept her promise to Jacques Bertrand. Each time she saw me, she offered new fragments of their story or, if my mother's fears were correct, the story she needed us to believe. I looked like him, had his eyes and his chin. Like my parents, my grandmother and the headmaster doted on me. When I returned to the States at the end of each August, I would try to ask my mother questions, to better piece things together but she would only shut herself in her room, rub perfume across her upper lip, lie on her back, her eyes covered with a cool washcloth.

When I was thirteen, the headmaster drove my grandmother and me to their beach property in Montrouis for the afternoon. Just before leaving New York for the summer, I had celebrated my Bat Mitzvah. The three of us sang along to konpa, and the adults listened to me chattering from the backseat. It was a good day. I longed for my mother to know there was so much joy to be found in the country of her birth. As we pulled into a gas station, beggars suddenly swarmed our car, a throbbing mass of dark, shiny faces and limbs needing more than we could possibly give. There was a man with one leg and one old, wooden crutch. His face was disfigured by a bulging tumor beneath his left eye. He planted his hands against the glass of the window, leering at me, the skin over the tumor rippling with his anger. It was the first time I understood the land of my mother's birth as a place run through with pain.

Each time I returned to New York and the comforts of home, I brought pictures and long letters and special spices—these affections, mother by proxy. My mother always took me for lunch, alone, at the Russian Tea Room the day following my return. She had me recount my trip in exhaustive detail, inhaling from a perfume-scented handkerchief every few minutes, carefully probing so as to get the clearest sense of how her mother was doing. Once in a while, I forgot myself and asked my mother why she didn't just go to Haiti to find out for herself. In those moments, she gave me a stern look. She said, "It is not easy to be a good daughter."

When I turned sixteen I went to summer camp in Western Massachusetts because I was young and silly. I wanted to do normal things. Haiti was too much work. I was tired of the heat and the smells and the inescapable poverty, how my sweaty limbs caught in mosquito netting, how I had to go to the well for water when the cistern wasn't working. I was sick of the loud hum of generators and tiny lizards clinging to window screens and the way everyone stared at me and called me la mulatte. Summer camp was a largely disappointing experience. I was a city girl and the Berkshires were far too rural for me. I wasn't any kind of Jewish the other girls at the camp could understand. I spent the summer sitting on the lakeshore reading, lamenting that I could have been at a real beach in the Caribbean with people who loved me and looked like me. It would be ten years before I returned to Haiti.

The next summer, my father took me to Tel Aviv. He showed me the apartment where he grew up in Ramat Aviv. He showed me his parents' graves, told me how much they would have loved me. I saw all kinds of people who did indeed look like me, who didn't laugh at my stuttered Hebrew. We spent a week on a kibbutz, my father in his linen shirt and shorts, tanned, laughing, home. I felt a real sadness for my mother who couldn't take such joy in the land of her birth. We went to the beach. We went to Jaffa and looked toward the sea and Andromeda's Rock. We cried at the Wailing

Wall. I understood Haiti was not the only place in the
world run through with pain.

The year after I graduated from law school, the headmaster died. I called my grandmother to ask how she
was doing. She said, "I have been a good wife." She was
ready to return to Jacques Bertrand. I told my mother
we had to go see her mother. She was lying on her
bed, rubbing perfume across her upper lip. She had not
taken news of the headmaster's death well. He was the
only father she ever knew. She turned to me and said,
"This is my home, where I am needed." I said, "You
are needed elsewhere," and she waved a hand limply,
conceding the point.

My father prescribed my mother some Valium,
and the three of us flew to Port-au-Prince. By the time
we landed, my mother was sufficiently sedated. As we
disembarked and walked into the terminal, she dream-
ily asked, "Are we there?" My grandmother and her
driver were waiting for us. I inhaled sharply as I saw
her for the first time in a decade. She was impossibly
small, a frail figure, her dark flesh much looser now,
her features hollowed, her white hair swept atop her
head in a loose bun. She and my mother stood inches

apart and stared at each other. My grandmother took her daughter's face in her hands, nodded. That night, in our hotel, I heard my mother whisper to my father that she could hardly breathe but for the smell of blood.

After we had spent a few days in the capital helping my grandmother settle her affairs and visiting the headmaster's grave, she was ready to return to Jacques Bertrand. Despite our demand she stay in the capital or return to the States with us, my grandmother was resolute. We drove across the country to Ouanaminthe on the only passable road. It took hours and by the time we arrived, we were all tired, sweaty, sore, and irritable. Ouanaminthe was not the city it had once been. It was a sad, hopeless place, crumbling buildings everywhere, paint peeling from billboards, the streets crowded with people, each person wanting and needing more than the last. Most of the roads had gone to mud from recent flooding. The air was stifling and pressed down on us uncomfortably. As we stood in the courtyard in front of the small concrete house my grandmother had purchased, men hanging from a passing Tap Tap leered at us. My father stood in front of me, glaring. My mother rubbed her forehead and asked my father for another Valium.

My mother and her mother kept to themselves for the first few days, huddled together, trying to make up for nearly thirty years of separation. There was no room for my father and me in what they needed from one another. On the second night, I went to a local bar where everyone stared as I took a seat. I drank watery rum and Coke until my face and boredom felt numb. I danced to Usher with a man named Innocent. When I sneaked back into my grandmother's house, I found her sitting in the dark. She nodded to me but said nothing. On the third night, the moon was high and bright, casting its pale light over and through everything. I lay beneath mosquito netting in a tank top and boxers, one arm over my head, one arm across my stomach, my body feeling open and loose. I listened to the sounds of everyone else sleeping. I tried to understand the what and why of where we were.

Just as I was on the verge of drifting asleep, I heard a scratching at the door and sat up, pulling the sheets around me. My grandmother appeared in the doorway. She curled her bent fingers, beckoning. Slowly, I stretched myself out of bed, pulled on a pair of jeans, and flip-flops. I found my grandmother by the front door. My mother was standing next to her, fidgeting, shifting from one foot to the other, clutching at her perfume-scented handkerchief. "What's wrong?" I asked. My grandmother smiled in the darkness. "Come with us," she said.

We walked nearly a mile to the banks of the Massacre River, my grandmother pressing her hand against the small of my mother's back. In the distance, we could see soldiers keeping watch at the checkpoint, their cigarettes punctuating the darkness. I heard hundreds of frightened people who looked like me splashing through the water, searching for safety and then, silence. My grandmother climbed down the damp, steep riverbank, my mother warning her mother to be careful. She waved for us to join her. I slipped out of my sandals, took my mother's hand, helped her into the river. We stood in a shallow place. I curled my toes in the silt of the riverbed and shivered. I had pictured the river as a wide, yawning, and bloody beast, but where we stood, the river flowed weakly. The waters did not run deep. It was just a border between two geographies of grief.

My grandmother pointed down. The hem of her dressing gown floated around her. "Here," she said softly.

My mother's shoulders shook but she made no sound. She gripped my arm. "I cannot breathe," she said. Then she dropped to her knees, curled into herself. She said, "I must know the truth."

I knelt behind her. I held her, tried to understand her. I said, "You can breathe." My grandmother said, "You know the only truth that matters." Again I heard hundreds of frightened people splashing through the water, keening, reaching for something that could never be reached. The ground beneath us trembled from the heavy footsteps of roving soldiers. I smelled their sweat and their confused, aimless anger.

We knelt there for a long while. My grandmother stood, whispering the story of how she came to know and remember Jacques Bertrand until her words dried on her lips. I stroked my mother's hair gently, waited for her breathing to slow, her back rising into my chest with a melancholy cadence. We mourned until morning. The sun rose high. Bright beams of light spread over and through us. The sun burned so hot it dried the river itself, turned the water into light. We were left kneeling in a bed of sand and bones. I started crying. I could not stop. I cried to wash us all clean.

# Lacrimosa

M arise thought she knew things about tears. When she was a little girl in Port-au-Prince, her father would listen to Mozart's Requiem while their neighbors danced to konpa and American rock and roll and R & B. Their small two-room home would fill with the melancholy of earnest choral voices and string instruments. Whenever the Lacrimosa sequence began, her father would close his eyes and hold a hand high in the air. Everyone would still. The music was so beautiful Marise knew she was feeling everything that could ever be felt. Then the government was overthrown again and again and again and mouths grew hungry and an even thicker maze of wires began stretching from house to house, each family stealing power from here and there. Walking down alleys, you could no longer see the sky and then it was time for the generators with their loud angry hum making everything thick with the smell of diesel. Her father put the turntable away. There was nothing left to feel.

When the UN soldier first came to her door with his brown skin and baby blue bulletproof vest, he said his name was Carlos Rocha from Veli Velha, Brazil. He held his helmet in the crook of his arm, his long rifle slung over his shoulder. Fat beads of sweat rolled down his face. He had money, a slow lazy grin, and curly black hair. He smiled at her only child. Carlos Rocha gently squeezed the boy's cheek between the calluses of his soldier hands. He asked if she cooked, what she charged for her spare room. His grin widened, revealing dimples. She smiled back, nervous, named her price. Everything in Port-au-Prince had a price.

The soldier moved in. Every night, he returned to Marise's well-kept home, complained about the heat, the heavy air, the trash everywhere, the dark shiny people throwing rocks and bottles and angry words. He ate her food. He shared her bed, touched her body with his soldier hands; he filled her and frightened her and she felt something she didn't understand. She learned about lachrymatory agents, how chemical compounds

were designed for the express purpose of stimulating
the corneal nerves to draw tears and inflict pain. He
told her how his unit was once locked in a bunker filled
with tear gas. The soldiers tried not to breathe or cry,
the jowls of their cheeks quivering uncontrollably until
their chests threatened to explode and finally they
sobbed not because of the burning in their eyes, nose,
and throat but because of the frailty of feeling everything at once. Marise sang songs to comfort the soldier
after his long days patrolling dark, dangerous places.
She learned his words. He learned hers. She worried.

It did not take long for Marise to forget that Carlos
Rocha was a man on a mission. He was far from his
home. He would not stay. The warmth of her body,
the way she welcomed him inside her, the taste of her
skin were all things he would walk away from. He kept
a well-oiled gun beneath her bed, carried it every day,
and once in a while he shot he fired he hurt he killed.
She forgot all this until one day, her boy sat in front of
their small concrete home, tears streaming down his
face as he stacked spent tear gas canisters as high as his
little arms could reach. When the boy felt his mother's
shadow over him, he looked up with his bright shining

eyes, holding a canister in each chubby fist. He said, "Look Mama, I made!" She remembered what was and what would not be. She pulled her child into her arms. She felt nothing but the bitterness of her son's tears on her tongue.

# The Harder
# They Come

We were told lots of things about The Americans—they want our skin bronze and our teeth white and gleaming and our shirts cut low. The Americans want us to be impressed by the size of their cruise ship and other such things. The Americans want us to speak English, but not too well. The Americans want us to smile and flatter.

Every week, we stand, perfectly groomed in a perfect line. We watch as the cruise ship slowly pulls into port. Before long, the pier fills with The Americans—some pale, some tan, mostly large and red-faced. The women wear ill-fitting bikinis and wraps and sundresses. The men wear Hawaiian shirts and board shorts and khaki shorts and tank tops. Their faces are covered with large, black sunglasses. They talk loudly. They walk slowly. As they near us, they look up at the large sign that reads, "Welcome to Labadee." They see us and say, "The local color here is just so pretty."

We serve them drinks and local foods and sell them "handmade crafts from local artisans" that arrived on another boat from China.

The Americans rent Jet Skis and shout to each other as they bounce over waves. Their skin bronzes and burns. The Americans are happy.

They drink and drink and drink and get louder and happier. They ask us to take their pictures and they point their cameras at us so when they return home, they can have friends over for wine to show off all the dangerous places they have been.

The Americans apply suntan lotion and bathe in the sun, stretching their bodies on striped chaise lounges, and as they bake, they fill the air with the sickly sweet smell of coconut oil. They listen to music and read glossy magazines and try to decide what they want for dinner back on the boat and complain about the thick, humid air.

They say they quite like this Haiti, so clean and calm, so pleasant, not at all like on CNN. The Americans ask questions but rarely listen to the answers. Beyond the pier and the heat of the white sand beach with the striped chaise lounges and the thatched huts with brightly colored roofs there is a thick line of lush palm trees and behind the lush palm trees is a very tall fence lined with barbed wire separating this Haiti from that Haiti. The Americans never ask to see that Haiti. The Americans know that Haiti is there.

The Americans, the men, they like us and want us. They think we too are for sale as part of the Hispaniola experience. They offer us their American dollars and expect us to be impressed by the likeness of Andrew Jackson. We prefer the countenance of Benjamin Franklin. The Americans grab our asses and whisper in our ears, leaving their hot, boozy breath on our skin. The less original among them say things like, "Voulez-vous couchez avec moi?" in heavy, awkward French, overenunciating each word. Some of us are indeed for sale or want to know what it would be like with a man with such pale skin or we are bored or we just don't care. We tell The Americans to follow us. We walk down the hot sandy beach slowly, shaking our hips and they ogle us and they say vulgar things we pretend not to hear. We walk until we can no longer see the pier, can no longer hear the laughter or the sharp hum of Jet Skis or the haggling for local crafts. We sneak behind a rocky embankment or a small thicket of palm trees or a deserted section of shaded beach.

The men, The Americans, they don't fill our heads with romantic ideas. There are no tender moments. The Americans bite our bare shoulders and squeeze our brown breasts in their meaty hands. They groan as they tell us to get on our knees, take them in our mouths. They ask us if we like it. We pretend not to speak English. We whisper silly things in French. We try not to laugh which sounds like a moan and that, The Americans adore. They fuck us from behind with our hands and cheeks pressed against the burning rocks. They fuck us behind the market or against the fence beyond the thick line of lush palm trees. They never take long. They never say thank you. The Americans, however, always come.

# All Things
# Being Relative

The copper country of Michigan's Upper Peninsula is a forgotten place. The land is vast and densely forested, filled with ghosts and skeletons wandering through the industrial ruin. In the summer, the U.P. is breathtaking and irresistible; in the winter, blanketed by snow upon snow, ice, and sand, the U.P. is unforgiving, inhospitable, inescapable.

Copper once reigned. There were mines, rich with ore, and men ready, willing, able to pull that bounty from the earth. The mine owners prospered. They built grand homes atop hills, had buildings named after them. The men who worked for these mine owners did not prosper as much but they owned homes of their own and they fed their families and on Sundays they went to church to thank the god who provided all good gifts.

Progress is not kind and human nature cannot resist the lure of possibility. Where once it was man who pulled the copper from the enriched soil of the Upper Peninsula, then it was machine, and then there was no need for any of it, and then there was nothing left.

There is a beauty to be found in an abandoned mine. There is also a profound sadness. Stone walls decaying into awkward angles. Machines rusted in motion. Grasses grown wild, encroaching on all things.

Old houses, haunted by miners with nothing to mine, don't fade away. They fall. They slump to their knees. They bow their heads.

We get the news here in upper Michigan—the frenzied accounts of recessions and depressions and unemployment. Things have changed, we're told. It's a new world and a new economy. People are hungry, tired, sick, poor. There is no respite—no way to satisfy our hunger or rejuvenate our spirits, heal our wounds or change our fortunes. We laugh, bitterly. This is not news.

My parents were born in Haiti, the first free black nation in the world.

It is an island of contradictions.

The sand is always warm. The water is so clear-blue bright that it is sometimes painful to behold. The art and music are rich, textured, revelatory, ecstatic. The sugarcane is raw and sweet.

And yet. What most people think they know is this: Haiti is the poorest country in the Western Hemisphere. Her people eat mud cakes. There is no infrastructure—no sewer system, no reliable roads, erratic electricity. Women are not safe. Disease cannot be cured. Violence cannot be quelled. The land is eroding. The sky is falling.

Freedom, it seems, has a price. We are defined by what we are not and what we do not have.

We get American news in Haiti, too, via CNN, beamed down from satellites. We hear about these recessions and depressions, the unemployment, how things have changed. In the background, we listen to the grinding hum of the generator; perhaps, in the distance, gunshots as UN peacekeepers and roving gangs skirmish. We laugh. We marvel at such good news. The bitter taste burns.

# Gracias, Nicaragua y Lo Sentimos

Nicaraguenses, nosotros Haitianos lo sentimos pero no queremos más el titulo del país más pobre en el hemisferio occidental. Le damos las gracias. El deshonor ahora es el suyo.

You should know this: every news story ever written or aired in perpetuity, whether on Euronews, Univision, ESPN or ABC, CNN, CBS, FOX or NBC, will begin and end referring to your beloved land as the poorest country in the Western Hemisphere. You are what you have not.

You will hear these words until you are sick to your stomach, until you no longer recognize su tierra, until you start to believe the news stories are true, that nothing else matters, that si no puedes comprar cosas que no necesitas, tu no existes, tu no cuentas, tu no mereces respeto.

It won't matter if the story is about Nicaraguan art or the food, the music or your people. It could be a story about wages or natural disasters, unrest in the countryside, the latest telenovela, or escándalo político.

Por ejemplo, a blond American reporter could be interviewing a famous Nicaraguan children's author. Her very first question undoubtedly will be, "What's it like coming from the poorest nation in the Western Hemisphere?"

Just know, the poor author will be left standing with her brightly illustrated book, full of ideas, vim, and vigor, eager to discuss historias para los niños, and instead she will have to call upon the political science class she slept through in college to make do in her new role as political correspondent.

At least in hearing this, you know what to expect. You might also take comfort en el conocimiento that it likely won't take long for Ayiti to regain her place. El deshonor siempre ha sido nuestro.

# The Dirt
# We Do Not Eat

Once or twice a month, Elsa in Cap-Haïtien receives a letter from her cousin Sara in Miami. The letter is thick with news and US dollars and promises of a better life, a better place, a better time, better things.

I wish you could see South Beach, Sara writes. The men are more beautiful than the women. They all wear makeup and fine clothes. The beach is not like home. It is crowded. It is dirty. After work my friends and I, we run along the water barefoot. We drink straight from bottles of wine. We eat McDonald's and other good food that is also bad. They put so much salt on the french fries for hours you can suck the grains from your fingers, feel them on your lips.

Elsa saves these letters in a tin box she keeps beneath the narrow bed she shares with her boyfriend who she pretends is her husband even though he has another woman on the side.

My dearest cousin, Elsa writes back, South Beach sounds like a dream. I have never tasted wine but worry not. We still have our rum. You should know Christian is up to his old tricks, he won't work, he won't stay, and yet he does not leave. I think of you often. I wait for you to steal me away.

Elsa misses Sara. She does. She hates Sara. She does. She hates the letters, the news, the promises, the lies. She hates hearing about air-conditioning and water always running cold, safe to drink from the faucet, and TV shows about strippers and millionaires and more.

Is it true Haitians are eating mud pies? Sara wants to know. Has it been so long since I've been home that the land itself sustains us? Last night I ate Dairy Queen. The ice cream reminded me of the poem we read when we were in secondaire about plums in the icebox, so cold and so sweet. I will never be able to enjoy another treat if it is true that all we have left is the ground at our feet, wet with water, a little salt, squeezed between our hands, baked in the hot sun, dry in our mouths.

Those left behind have heard these stories on Euronews and on Radio Metropole because one eager journalist saw what he wanted to see, saw an old woman at the side of the road, squatting over her pies, her bare knees peeking out from the folds of her skirt.

Ma chère cousine, writes Elsa. I read your letter while walking on white sand burning my bare feet. I looked out at the water so clear blue it hurt my eyes. Last night, maman made us griot and diri ak pwa and Christian who can smell a good meal from between a woman's thighs finally came home. The three of us ate together and we laughed. There wasn't much food but what there was, was enough. I'll tell you this. We do not enjoy as much food as perhaps once we did. When Christian goes to get rice from MINUSTAH, he must take his gun, three friends. Some mornings we wake, our stomachs empty, our stomachs angry, but never do we look to the ground beneath our feet with longing in our mouths. We chew on our pride. The dirt we do not eat.

# What You Need
# to Know About
# a Haitian Woman

When his wife was a young girl, she was playing with a young chick in the yard, chasing after it, laughing, having fun. When the mother hen realized her child was being teased, she ran across the dusty yard and began pecking at his not-yet-wife's legs. His future mother-in-law, upon seeing her child being hen-pecked, ran outside, raised the mother hen in the air, and snapped its neck. Later, she had the chicken prepared for dinner. She said it was the best meal she ever ate. When the mother hen's chicks grew up, she killed them, too. The point, the Haitian father will then say to a potential suitor, is this: You don't need to worry about him. You need to worry about the mother.

# Of Ghosts
# and Shadows

I am watching my lover, Amèlie, move through the market sifting through items neither of us can hope to afford. It is stinking hot, the kind of hot where it feels like even my eyeballs are sweating and I want nothing more than to jump into the salty water of the ocean for respite. I am watching my lover because it is too dangerous to do anything but watch. Her face is thin and drawn but when her fingers dance across a trinket she likes, her eyes light up and the muscles in her shoulders relax. I imagine that she is imagining what it would be like to own these petty items she covets. There are a few tourists in the market, walking around confused, as if they read the wrong brochure. Most Americans come to Haiti expecting it to be like Aruba or St. Kitts. They lump all of these small islands into one paradise where libations flow freely and cabana boys are waiting to attend to their every need. Unfortunately for them, the cabana boys have all fled the country and there is no ice to cool their drinks.

Amèlie and I have known each other since we were children. Our mothers are best friends and together, we watched our fathers taken away for supporting free elections, we watched our brothers disappear into the countryside or the ocean, and we watched each other. We always watched each other. Once, as we sat on her front porch drinking mango juice, holding the cool glasses to our foreheads between sips, she turned to me and said, "Sometimes, Marie Françoise, you are the only thing in this world I care to see."

A gaggle of schoolchildren noisily push their way past me, and just looking at them makes me want to cry. They are so young, not so innocent, and they too want things they cannot have. Amèlie looks up and smiles at me. No one else could recognize it as a smile, but I know. Her eyelids are raised, lips slightly curled at the edges, her thumb grazing her chin. I cock my head to the side and pretend to be interested in a box of Corn Flakes selling for thirteen dollars. I smooth one eyebrow and draw my finger down my cheek. This is my way of smiling at her, telling her that I wish I could touch her face, hold her hand as we shop, whisper futile fantasies of what we wish was but cannot be.

Slowly, I move toward her, ignoring the bony elbows, gaunt faces, tired old women sucking their lips. My heart pounds and with each step, the sharp twinge between my thighs melts into a gentle throb. I should stay away, but I am feeling rebellious today. I enjoy torturing myself with this dance of being so close yet so far. When I am finally next to her, I carefully inspect a handful of patterned beads with my left hand, my right loosely by my side, two fingers reaching toward the worn pink fabric of her dress, one of only three she owns. She leans into me and I can feel the light pressure of her thigh against my finger, her bare arm against mine.

She turns and I can feel her staring at me. I force myself to look forward but it feels like she is reaching inside my body with her eyes, reaching past skin, bone, and blood to my heart. I slide my fingers upward, along the round edges of her hip to her waist. In another time, or another place, or if I were another person, I would stand behind her, graze the back of her neck with my lips. I would wrap my arms around her for a moment of comfort before taking her hand to continue strolling through the market. But since we are here and now, I step away as I notice a group of young, angry men walking toward us. I doubt that there is any particular reason for their anger. It is the anger that most men feel these days; they are angry about their impotence and their desires and their reality. It is an anger we all feel. But it is an anger only men can freely express.

I start walking in the other direction and though I want to turn around and whisper *I love you,* I keep walking. On days like today, I think I could walk until the muscles in my legs burned in protest, until I drifted into the ocean, until I walked into that time and place where Amèlie and I could be together, out in the open.

For now, we are women who don't exist. We are less than shadows, more than ghosts. We're the wayward relatives neighbors gossip about in hushed, horrified tones. We are the women people ignore because two women loving each other is an American thing—not the sort of behavior god-fearing island folk would engage in. There are a few people who live openly, men mostly, artists who are indulged in their bright-colored sashaying about town because their work is so brilliant. But even they meet with contempt now and then:

an insult hurled here, a sharp rock thrown there. And when they get sick, they are greeted with smug smiles, a harsh reminder of all good things, as their bodies waste to nothing.

Amèlie and I were caught once, when I was twenty-three and she was twenty-two. It was late at night and we met in the dark shadows between our houses. Our mothers were asleep; our neighbors were asleep. It was a moment when we were the only two women in the world and we felt a certain freedom—a freedom to do as we pleased. Even beneath the cover of night it was so hot that we were sweating. There are nights in Haiti when it feels possible that the moon burns just as hot as the sun. She was wearing a T-shirt and old sandals. I was wearing my housecoat, the top three buttons open. We clasped hands and sank into the darkest part of that dark space and we traced each other's faces with our fingers as if in the space of the few hours since we last saw each other, perhaps our features had changed.

I ran my tongue from the tip of her chin to the hollow just beneath her throat. I tasted the salt of sweat and could feel her breath humming just beneath the surface of her skin. We said nothing, but there was no need for words. Everything that could possibly be said had already been spoken between us over the course of so many years. She clasped the back of my neck and lifted my head, bringing my lips to hers, and she kissed me so hard, I imagined she could swallow me whole. Our lips were so dry and cracked I tasted blood. My tongue pushed past her lips, running over the sharp edges of her teeth, meeting with hers. And then she pushed me lower, pulling her T-shirt over her narrow shoulders. I took her breasts into my hands, and the soft mounds of flesh spilled through my fingers. Amèlie whispered only one word, "Please," so I laid her on the ground, my hands greedily spreading her thighs.

The earth beneath our bodies was warm, inviting, generous. And then, we heard a gasp, and I knew if I moved, my heart would fall from my chest and into the ground. I knew all my fears were about to come to pass. I have had many such moments. Amèlie scrambled away from me, reaching for her T-shirt, wrapping her arms around her chest as if she could disappear if she sat ever so still. Slowly, I turned my head and saw my mother beneath a thin shaft of moonlight, and the look on her face was so horrified, so distant, I hardly recognized her. She turned and walked away. We never

spoke of it—neither me and my mother nor me and my
lover—but Amèlie and I never met in the dark between
our houses ever again.

Now, five years later, when we want to make love
we steal away to a friend's house when we can, or we
get together once in a while with other people like us,
women and men who are also less than shadows, more
than ghosts. They are sad little affairs, our get-togethers,
on Saturday nights in the back room of someone's house
in Port-au-Prince. The rum is watered down. We have
to pay ten dollars to get in, and the entire time, we try
to pretend we are in New York or Miami or Montreal,
at a club with friends. We try to show each other affec-
tion. We try to pretend we aren't staring at the doorway,
afraid we'll be caught. And Amèlie and I will steal to
the bathroom, dark and dank, with little room to move.
We'll fumble with our clothing, and shove our hands
between each other's thighs, kissing for so long that we
start breathing for each other, trying to extract as much
pleasure from our bodies as possible before we have to
return home.

On a strangely cool December evening not too
long ago, a group of men, boys really, raided our private party. Amèlie and I were sitting on a couch, our

arms around each other, when five men came through the front door. We could smell drink on them—we could smell hate. Albèrt, a friend of ours was by the door, and they grabbed him by his shirt, shoving him against the wall, saying the crudest, cruelest things they could. One of them, tall, fair-skinned, with wide features, threw the stereo on the floor and began beating it with a baseball bat. But for some reason, the music played on. The air was filled with their taunts and the tinny music playing. "Faggots," the man with the bat sneered. For a moment, we froze, eleven of us, hoping our passivity would bring the moment to an end. And then we were running through the house and out the back door, away from that place. We knew we were cowards but we didn't dare look back. The next day, we heard that Albèrt was in the hospital with three broken ribs, a broken hand, and a chorus of bruises. I mourned for his pain. But I didn't want that to be me, and I didn't want that to be Amèlie. It was simply one more shame to bear. The same could be said for all of us. But we continued to meet, continued to defy *the rules*, because we knew that such stolen moments are the one small thing we have in this big, big world.

When I arrive home, my mother is in bed asleep. For the past several years, she has spent most of her time sleeping, and her slumber is understandable. I stand in her doorway, listening to the sound of her breathing. It is shallow and timid. The wrinkles in her face are sharp. She looks so relaxed, so at peace, that I can't bear to wake her, disturb her stolen moment. And to wake her would do just that. I see the pain in her face when she looks at me. It is the sorrow of living with a daughter she loves but doesn't want. There are times when I think of settling down with a man, any man. It would please my mother to no end. But then I think of the scent of Amèlie's neck and the flutter of her fingers over mine. And I know that despite the unbearable distance between us, I would not have things any other way. Neither would she.

In the kitchen, I prepare myself a mug of café au lait, and though the air is hot, even indoors, I hold my face over the steam, my pores opening. From the window I can see directly into Amèlie's house. I sit there, and wait to watch her return home from the market. Her mother waves from the porch and I offer her a shy smile, a careful wave, and then I look away before my face says too much. I sit for hours and I think of the last time Amèlie and I made love, how fleeting it was, how hungry it has left me. I think of her sticky thighs rubbing against each other as she walks and I think of her in the market, and the warmth of her thigh pressing against the edge of my fingertips—so many stolen moments.

The first time we made love was a shy and awkward affair. I was nineteen, she had just turned eighteen, and as we walked home from school, the cracked pavement burning through the thin soles of our shoes, I grabbed her hand with mine, clenching it so tightly my knuckles turned white. She stopped and stared at me. I opened my mouth, but there were no words. But there were words, I simply didn't know how to wrap my lips around them. In the distance, a lone Toyota ambled toward us, but I closed my eyes, leaned into her, and brushed my lips across hers. I traced the arch of her eyebrow with one finger, and then I ran away, trying not to cry. She called after me, but when I turned around, she wasn't following, so I kept running, off the road and through a cane field, ignoring the brambles that scratched my skin, until I reached my house. My mother clutched her chest when she saw me, but I shook my head and retired to my bedroom where I sat on the cool concrete floor in a corner, my arms wrapped around my knees, rocking back and forth.

Moments later, there was a light knock on the door.

"Go away," I said hoarsely, but the wooden door slowly creaked open, and there Amèlie stood, pale, lips pursed. She stepped inside my room and closed the door behind her.

"Why did you do that?" she asked.

I lowered my head, staring at the floor. She moved closer, close enough for me to smell sweat and the lingering scent of her perfume. She knelt, her knees pressed against mine, and she cupped my face between her hands and in that moment she was holding the whole of me.

"Why did you do that?" she asked again.

I looked up. "I feel things I am not supposed to feel. I want things I am not supposed to want."

"How do you know that?"

I laughed, bitterly. "If you knew, you would turn around. You would never look upon me again."

"Do you not know me at all?"

"It is not as simple as that."

She took my hand in hers, held it between her breasts. Her skin thrummed lightly through her shirt and my fingers trembled. It took all my self-control not to move my hand mere inches to the right or left. And then, her hand covering mine, she slid my hand under her shirt, up the smooth of her stomach and cupped it around her breast. I sighed a heavy sigh, enjoying the weight of her in the palm of my hand. I had imagined that moment for so long, lying in bed alone on dark, humid nights, that I felt a sharp, intense pain between my eyes, and for a moment, the world went white.

"Perhaps it is that simple," she said.

A single cry escaped the dryness of my throat. I kissed her chin, her neck, pulled her shirt over her shoulders as my mouth fumbled lower. She held me to her, her fingers drawing small circles against the back of my neck. I could hear my mother shuffling around in the kitchen and my heart pounded as I prayed she wouldn't disturb us. I slid my hand beneath the elastic waistband of Amèlie's skirt. She remained silent and kneeling, but she parted her thighs, pressed herself against my fingers though I had no clear idea of what I was doing. Like a distant echo I could hear my mother calling me to dinner, asking Amèlie if she wanted to join us. I could not breathe.

It is hours past dark when Amèlie finally comes home. As she stands on the threshold of her house, she looks at me, sees me in the shadows, and changes her mind, making her way to my house. I greet her at the door and she looks so sad, so hollow, that I open my arms and she tumbles against my chest, perching her head against my shoulder.

"I cannot sleep alone tonight," she whispers. "I simply cannot."

I lift her chin with a finger, look into her eyes. "We could call on Patricia, see if she'd let us spend the night there."

Amèlie shakes her head. "I want to sleep here in your . . . in our bed."

There are butterflies in my stomach. I did not realize until now that I have always wanted to hear her say those words. "My mother is here"

"I don't care, do you?"

I think of all the tiny pleasures we have denied ourselves over the years. I cannot deny her this one thing, the only thing she has ever asked of me. "Come," I say, leading her to the bedroom.

We tiptoe past my mother's bedroom; she is snoring now, but I do not bother to shut her door, nor do I shut mine. Amèlie's courage tonight, however blind it may be, makes me want to be just as brave. Her courage makes me wonder if we really have anything to fear—as if it is only ghosts and shadows forbidding our passion. She strips out of her clothes, as do I, and we crawl into my bed, which creaks beneath our weight. She lies on her back, I on my side.

She traces my lips with her thumb. Her smile is genuine. The depths of her light brown eyes are fathomless. I see wisdom there, fear, a little happiness, desire.

The tension between us is palpable. I wonder if Amèlie's mother knows where Amèlie is, what her daughter is doing. I exhale loudly. I did not realize I have been holding my breath.

"Shh," Amèlie says, pressing one finger to my lips. I think about how dangerous this is for us. I think about stones striking flesh. My mother could be standing in the doorway but I do not turn my head.

We lie down, together. She covers her hand with mine. I fall asleep before I can tell her I love her, listening to the sound of her beating heart and rushing blood. I cannot tell her that she should leave before dawn arrives. I am too tired and too satisfied to be afraid. In the morning, my mother will find us like this, limbs entangled, bodies as one, breathing each other's breath. My mother will think she is seeing ghosts or perhaps shadows. She will be right.

# A Cool,
# Dry Place

Yves and I are walking because even if his Citroën was working, petrol is almost seven dollars a liter. He is wearing shorts, faded and thin, and I can see the muscles of his thighs trembling with exhaustion. He worries about my safety, so every evening at six, he picks me up at work and walks me home, all in all a journey of twenty kilometers amid the heat, the dust, and the air redolent with exhaust fumes and the sweet stench of sugarcane. We try to avoid the crazy drivers who try to run us off the road for sport. We walk slowly, my pulse quickening as he takes my hand. Yves's hands are what I love best about him; they are callused and wrinkled, the hands of a much older man. At times, when he is touching me, I know there is wisdom in those hands.

We have the same conversation almost every day—what a disaster the country has become—but we cannot even muster the strength to say the word *disaster* because the word does not describe our lives. There is sadness in Yves's face that also defies description. It is an expression of ultimate sorrow, the reality of witnessing the country, the home you love, disappearing not into the ocean but into itself.

We stop at the market in downtown Port-au-Prince. Posters for Aristide and the Fanmi Lavalas are all over the place even though the elections, an exercise in futility, have come and gone. A vendor with one leg and swollen arms offers me a package of Tampax for twelve dollars, thrusting the crumpled blue-and-white box toward me. I ignore him as a red-faced American tourist begins shouting at us. He wants directions to the Hotel Montana, he is lost, his map of the city is wrinkled and torn and splotched with cola. "We are Haitian, not deaf," I say. The American smiles, relaxes into the comfort of his own language.

Yves rolls his eyes and pretends to be fascinated with an art vendor's wares. He has no tolerance for fat Americans. They make him hungry. Hunger reminds him of the many things he tries to ignore. Yves learned English in school. I learned from television—*I Love Lucy*, *The Brady Bunch*, and my favorite show, *The*

*Jeffersons*, with the little black man who walks like a
chicken. When I was a child, I would sit and watch
these shows and mimic the actors' words until I spoke
them perfectly. Now, as I tell the red-faced man the
wrong directions, because he has vexed me, I mouth
my words slowly, with what I hope is a flawless American accent. The man shakes my hand too hard, and
thrusts five gourdes into my sweaty palm. Yves sucks
his teeth as the man walks off and tells me to throw the
money away, but I stuff the faded bills inside my bra.
We continue to walk around, pretending we can afford
to buy something sweet or something nice.

When we get home, the heat threatens to suffo-
cate us. It always does. The air-conditioning window
unit is not working, because it has been defeated by
the on and off of daily power outages. The air is thick
and refuses to move. I look at the rivulets of sweat
streaming down Yves's dark face. I want to run away
to someplace cool and dry. My mother has prepared
dinner, boiled plantains and legumes, a beef and
green bean stew. She is weary, sweating, bent, nearly
broken. She doesn't speak to us as we enter, nor do
we speak to her. There is nothing any of us can say
that hasn't already been said. She stares and stares at

the black-and-white photo of my father, a man I have little recollection of. He was murdered by the Makoute, the secret military police, when I was only five years old. Late at night, I dream of my father being dragged from our home, of his body beaten as he was thrown into the back of a large green military truck. He was the lucky one. Sometimes, my mother stares at my father so hard that her eyes glaze over, and she starts rocking back and forth. I look at Yves. I know should anything happen to him, it will be me holding his picture, remembering what was and will never be. I understand our capacity to love.

We eat quickly and after, Yves washes the dishes outside. My stomach still feels empty. I rest my hand over the slight swell of my belly. I want to complain I am still hungry, but I do not. I cannot add to their misery. I catch Yves staring at me through the dirty window as he dries his hands. He always looks at me in such a way that I know his capacity to love equals mine. His eyes are wide, lips parted slightly as if the words *I love you* are forever resting on the tip of his tongue. He smiles, but looks away quickly as if there is an unspoken rule forbidding such impossible moments of joy. Sighing, I stand and kiss my mother on the forehead, gently rubbing her shoulders. She pats my hand and I retire to the bedroom Yves and I share. I wait. I think about his teeth on my neck and the weight of his body pressing me into our bed. Sex is one of the few pleasures we have left. It is dark when Yves finally comes to bed. As he crawls under the sheets, I can smell rum on his breath. I lie perfectly still until he nibbles my earlobe.

Yves chuckles softly. "I know you are awake, Gabi."

I smile in the darkness and turn toward him. "I always wait for you."

He gently rolls me onto my stomach and kneels behind me, removing my panties as he kisses the small of my back. His hands crawl along my spine, and again I can feel their wisdom as he takes an excruciating amount of time to explore my body. I arch toward him as I feel his lips against the backs of my thighs and one of his knees parting my legs. I try and look back at him but he nudges my head forward and enters me in one swift motion. I inhale sharply, shuddering, a moan trapped in my throat. Yves begins moving against me, moving deeper and deeper inside me, and before I give myself over, I realize that the sheets are torn between my fingers and I am crying.

Later, Yves is wrapped around me, his sweaty chest clinging to my sweaty back. He holds my belly in his hands and I can feel the heat of his breath against the back of my neck.

"We should leave," he murmurs. "So that one day, I can hold you like this and feel our child living inside you."

I sigh. We have promised each other that we will not bring a child into this world and it is but one more sorrow heaped onto a mountain of sorrows we share. "How many times will we have this conversation? We'll never have enough money for the plane tickets."

"We'll never have enough money to live here, either."

"Perhaps we should just throw ourselves in the ocean." Yves stiffens and I squeeze his hand. "I wasn't being serious."

"Some friends of mine are taking a boat to Miami week after next."

This is another conversation we have too often. Many of our friends have tried to leave on boats. Some have made it, most have not, and too many have turned back when they realized the many miles between Haiti and Miami are not so few as the space on the map implies. "They are taking a boat to the middle of the ocean where they will surely die."

"This boat will make it," Yves says confidently. "A priest is traveling."

I close my eyes. I try to breathe, yearning for just one breath of fresh air. "Because God has done so much to help us here on land?"

"Don't talk like that." He is silent for a moment. "I told them we would be going, too."

I turn around and try to make out his features beneath the moon's shadows.

Yves grips my shoulders. Only when I wince does he let go. "This is the only thing that does make sense. Agwé will see that we make it to Miami and then we can go to South Beach and Little Haiti and watch cable TV."

My upper lip curls in disgust. "You will put your faith in the same god that traps us on this godforsaken island?"

"If we go we might know, once in our lives, what it is like to breathe."

My heart stops and the room suddenly feels like a big echo. I can hear Yves's heart beating where mine is not. I can imagine what Yves's face might look like beneath the Miami sun. I will follow him wherever he goes.

When I wake, I blink, covering my eyes as cruel shafts of sunlight cover our bodies. The sun never has mercy here. My mother is standing at the foot of the bed, clutching the black-and-white photo of my father.

"Mama?"

"The walls are thin," she whispers.

I stare at my hands. They have aged overnight. "Is something wrong?"

"You must go with Yves, Gabrielle," she says, handing me the picture of my father.

I stare at the picture trying to recognize the curve of my eyebrow or the slant of my nose in his features. When I look up, my mother is gone. For the next two weeks, I work and Yves spends his days doing odd jobs and scouring the city for the supplies he anticipates us needing. I go through the motions, straightening my desk, taking correspondence for my boss, gossiping with my coworkers. I am dreaming of Miami and places where Yves and I are never hungry or tired or scared or any of the other things we have become. I tell no one of our plans to leave, but I want someone to stop us, remind me of all the unknowns between here and there.

At night, we exhaust ourselves making frantic love. We no longer bother to stifle our voices. I do things I would have never considered before, things I have always wanted to do. There is a freedom in escape. Three nights before we are to leave, Yves and I are in bed, making love. We are neither loud nor quiet. Gently, Yves places one of his hands against the back of my head, urging me toward his cock. I resist at first, but he is insistent in his desire, his hand pressed harder, fingers tangling into my hair and taking firm hold. It becomes difficult to breathe but it also excites me, makes me wet as he carefully guides me, his hands gripping harder and harder, his breathing faster. Suddenly, he stops, roughly rolling me onto my chest, digging his fingers into my hips, pulling my ass into the air. I press my forehead against my arms, gritting my teeth. I allow Yves to enter me, whispering terrible words into the night as he rocks me. I feel so much pleasure, so much pain. The only thing I know is I want more—more of the dull ache and the sharp tingling, more of feeling like I will shatter into pieces if he pushes any further—more. Yves says my name, his voice so tremulous it makes my heart ache. It is nice to know he craves me in the same way, that my body clinging to his is a balm.

Afterward, we lie side by side, our limbs heavy, and Yves talks to me about South Beach with the confidence of a man who has spent his entire life in such a place: a place where rich people and beautiful people and famous people dance salsa at night and eat in fancy restaurants overlooking the water. He tells me of expensive cars that never break down and jobs for everyone, good jobs where he can use his engineering degree and I can do whatever I want. He tells me about Little Haiti, a neighborhood just like our country, only better because the air-conditioning always works and we can watch cable TV. The cable TV always comes up in our conversations. We are fascinated by its excess. He tells me all of this and I can feel his body next to mine, tense, almost twitching with excitement. Yves smiles more in two weeks than in the three years we have been married and the twenty-four years we have known each other and I smile with him because I need to believe this idyllic place exists. I listen even though I have doubts and I listen because I don't know what to say.

The boat will sail under the cover of night. On the evening of flight, I leave work as I always do, turning off all the lights and computers, smiling at the security guard, saying I will see everyone tomorrow. It is always when I am leaving work that I realize what an odd country Haiti is, with the Internet, computers, fax machines, and photocopiers in offices and the people who use them living in shacks with the barest of amenities. We are a people living in two different times. Yves is waiting for me as he always is, but today, he is wearing a nice pair of slacks and a button-down shirt, and the black shoes he wears to church. This is his best outfit, only slightly faded and frayed. The tie his father gave him is hanging from his left pocket. We don't talk on the way home. We only hold hands and he grips my fingers so tightly my elbow starts tingling. I say nothing, however, because I know that right now, Yves needs something to hold on to.

I want to steal away into the sugarcane fields we pass, ignoring the old men, dark, dirty, and sweaty as they wield their machetes. I want to find a hidden spot and beg Yves to take me, right there. I want to feel the soil beneath my back and the stalks of cane cutting my skin. I want to leave my blood on the land and my cries in the air before we continue our walk home, Yves's seed staining my thighs, my clothes and demeanor hiding an intimate knowledge. But such a thing is entirely inappropriate, or at least it was before all this madness began. My face burns as I realize what I am thinking and I start walking faster. I have changed so much in so short a time.

My mother has changed as well. I would not say she is happy, but the grief that normally clouds her features is missing, as if she slid out of her shadow and hid it someplace secret and dark. We have talked more in two weeks than in the past two years. We will write, and someday Yves and I will save enough money to bring my mother to Miami, but nothing will ever make up for the wide expanse between now and then.

By the time we reach our home, Yves and I are drenched in sweat. It is hot, yes, but this is a different kind of sweat. It reeks of fear and unspeakable tension. We stare at each other as we cross the threshold, each mindful of the fact that everything we are doing, we are doing for the last time. My mother is moving about the kitchen, muttering to herself. Our suitcases rest next to the kitchen table, and it all seems rather innocent, as if we are simply going to the country for a few days, and not across an entire ocean. I cannot rightly wrap my mind around the concept of crossing an ocean. All I know is this small island and the few feet of water I wade in when I am at the beach. Haiti is not a perfect home, but it is a home nonetheless.

Last night, Yves told me he never wants to return, that he will never look back, and lying in bed, my legs wrapped around his, my lips against the sharp of his collarbone, I burst into tears.

"Chère, what's wrong?" he asked, gently wiping my tears away with the soft pads of his thumbs.

"I don't like it when you talk like that."

Yves stiffened. "I love my country and I love my people, but I cannot bear the thought of returning to this place where I cannot work or feel like a man or even breathe. I mean you no insult when I say this, but you cannot possibly understand."

I wanted to protest, but as I lay there, my head pounding, I realized I probably couldn't understand what it would be like for a man in this country where men have so many expectations placed upon them that they can never hope to meet. There are expectations of women here, but it is, in some strange way, easier for us. It is in our nature, for better or worse, to do what is expected of us. And yet, there are times when it is not easier, times like that moment when I wanted to tell Yves we should stay and fight to make things better, stay with our loved ones, just stay.

I have saved a little money for my mother. It started with the five gourdes from the red-faced American, and then most of my paycheck and anything else I could come up with. This money will not make up for the loss of a daughter and a son-in-law but it is all I have. After we leave, she is going to stay with her sister in Petit-Goâve. I am glad for this. I could not bear the thought of her alone in this stifling little house, day after day.

I walk around the house slowly, memorizing each detail, running my hands along the walls, tracing each crack in the floor with my toes. Yves is businesslike and distant as he remakes our bed, fetches a few groceries for my mother, hides our passports in the lining of his suitcase. My mother watches us but we are all silent. I don't think any of us can bear to hear the sound of each other's voices. I don't think we know why. Finally, a few minutes past midnight, it is time. My mother clasps Yves's hands between hers, smaller, more brittle. She urges him to take care of me, of himself. His voice cracks as he assures her he will, that the three of us won't be apart long. She embraces me tightly, so tightly that again my arms go numb. I hold her, kissing the top of her head, promising to write as soon as we arrive in Miami, promising to write every single day, promising to send for her as soon as possible. I make so many promises I cannot promise to keep.

And then, we are gone. We do not look back. We do not cry. Yves carries our suitcases and quickly we make our way to a deserted beach where there are perhaps thirty others, looking as scared as us. There is a boat—large, and far sturdier than I had imagined. I have been plagued by nightmares of a boat made from weak and rotting wood, leaking and sinking into the sea, the only thing left behind, the hollow echo of screams. Yves greets a few of his friends, but stays by my side. "We're moving on up," I quip, and Yves laughs, loudly. I see the priest Yves promised would bless this journey. He is only a few years older than us. He appears painfully young. He has only a small knapsack and a Bible so worn it looks like the pages might fall apart at the lightest touch. His voice is quiet and calm as he ushers us onto the boat.

Belowdecks there are several small cabins, and Yves seems to know which one is ours. I realize Yves has spent a great deal of money to arrange this passage. He stands near the small bed, his arms shyly crossed over his chest, and I see an expression on his face I don't think I have ever seen before. He is proud, eyes watery, chin jutting forward. I will never regret this decision, no matter what happens to us. I have waited my entire life to see my husband like this. I see him for the first time.

Later, I am abovedecks, leaning over the railing, heaving what little food is in my stomach into the ocean. Even on the water, the air is hot and stifling. We are still close to Haiti. I had hoped the moment we set upon the ocean I would be granted one sweet breath of cool air. Yves is cradling me against him between my bouts of nausea, promising this sickness will pass, promising this is but a small price to pay. I am tired of promises, but they are all we have to offer. I tell him to leave me alone, and he is hurt, but I can't comfort him when I need to comfort myself. I brush my lips across his knuckles and tell him I'll meet him in our cabin soon. He leaves, reluctantly, and when I am alone, I close my eyes, inhaling the salt of the sea deep into my lungs, hoping that smelling this thick salty air is one more thing I am doing for the last time.

I think of my mother and father and I think that being here on this boat may well be the closest I will ever come to knowing my father, knowing what he wanted for his family. All I want is peace. I wipe my lips with the back of my hand, ignoring the strong taste of bile lingering in the back of my throat, I return belowdecks where I find Yves, sitting on the end of the bed, rubbing his forehead.

I place the palm of my hand against the back of his neck. It is warm and slick with sweat. "What's wrong?"

He looks up but not at me. "I'm worried about you."

I push him farther onto the bed and straddle his lap. He closes his eyes and I caress his eyelids with my fingers, enjoying the curl of his eyelashes and the way it tickles my skin. He is such a beautiful man, but I do not tell him this. He would take it the wrong way. It is a strange thing in some men, this fear of their own beauty. I lift his chin with one finger and trace his lips with my tongue. They are cracked but soft. His hands tremble but he grips my shoulders firmly. I am amazed at how little is spoken between us yet how much is said. We quickly slip out of our clothes and his thighs flex between mine. The sensation of his muscle against my flesh is a powerful one that makes my entire body tremble.

I slip my tongue between his lips and the taste of him is so familiar and necessary that I am suddenly weak. I fall into Yves, kissing him so hard I know my lips will be bruised in the morning. I want them to be. Yves pulls away first, drawing his lips roughly across my chin down to my neck, the hollow of my throat, practically gnawing at my skin with his teeth. I moan hoarsely, tossing my head backward. My neck throbs and I know that here too, there will be bruises. He sinks his teeth deeper into me and I can no longer see the fine line between pain and pleasure. But just as soon as I consider asking him to stop, he does, instead lathering the fresh wounds with the softness of his tongue, murmuring sweet and tender words. Such gentleness in the wake of such roughness leaves me shivering.

The weight of my breasts rests in Yves's hands and he lowers his lips to my nipples, suckling them. He looks up at me and it is unclear whether this is a moment of passion or a moment of comfort for him, for me. And then I cannot look at him so I rest my chin against the top of his head, my arms wrapped around him, my hips slowly rocking back and forth. I want him inside me, but I wait. This moment, whatever it is, demands patience.

Yves takes hold of my knees, spreading my legs wide and pushing them upward until they are practically touching my face. I rest my ankles against his shoulders and shudder as he buries inside me. I feel his pulsing length, his sweat falling onto my body, into my eyes, mingling with mine, the tension in his body as I claw at the wide stretch of black skin across his back. Tomorrow, he too will have bruises.

"Let go," I urge him.

Then, he is fucking me faster, harder. We are greedy. I cannot recognize him. I am thankful. I scream. The sound of it is a horrible thing. I can feel wetness trailing down the inside of my arm—Yves's tears. I am tender inside but I don't want Yves to ever stop.

With each stroke he takes me further away from the sorrows of home and closer to a cool, dry place.

# Acknowledgments

Stories in this collection previously appeared in the following publications: *decomP, Quick Fiction, Pinch, Guernica, Necessary Fiction, Weave, Caribbean Review of Books, trnsfr, Best Lesbian Erotica 2003,* and *Best American Erotica 2004. Ayiti* was originally published by Artistically Declined Press in 2011.

I am especially grateful to the editors of the fine magazines and anthologies where these pieces originally appeared. This book would not exist were it not for my parents, Michael and Nicole Gay, who raised my brothers and me to know and love where we come from. I write about Haiti and the Haitian American experience from a place of great privilege but also a place of great pride. Thanks also to Maria Massie, my indomitable agent. As always, I am grateful to my lovely friends who are so supportive of my work, so consistently. And thank you to my best friend, Tracy Gonzalez, who is probably bored with being thanked but will always be thanked, anyway. She knows why. (Also, she was right.)